The Dream Dealer

'Don't talk about my mother,' snapped Finn.

'Poor lad, so you don't have a real, live mother. I've got the finest Mother-Dream. Just the one for you. It's pricey but I couldn't take your money. It's your first ever dream. I'll give it to you free.'

The Dream Dealer knew his words were echoing in Finn's ears. 'Mother-Dream, Mother-Dream, Mother-Dream.' He knew the boy yearned to know what his mother looked like, longed to hear her voice, craved to touch her.

And there before him was a huge purple Ice-Dream.

'Ouch!' Finn yelped, shocked out of his trance by his mouse, Hercules, who had sunk his needle-like teeth into his thumb. 'What did you do that for?'

www.thedreamdealer.co.uk

The Dream Dealer

Marita Phillips

Cover illustration

Zdenko Basic and Manuel Sumberac

PUBLISHED BY NEVE PRESS

First published in Great Britain in 2011 by
Neve Press
53F Lancaster Gate, London W2 3NA

Reprinted 2011, 2012

British Library Cataloguing in Publication Data
A CIP catalogue record for this book is available from
the British Library

ISBN 978-0-9567530-0-7

First published in Great Britain by Neve Press 2011
Neve Press, 53F Lancaster Gate, London W2 3NA UK

Email: marita.phillips88@gmail.com
www.thedreamdealer.co.uk

Typeset by Chandler Book Design

Printed in England by
CPI Group (UK) Ltd, Croydon CR0 4YY

For my loving critics

Andrew

Aidan   Cosima   Galen

I have never come across anything like it. It is simple yet complicated, the plot is exceptional and fast moving. The characters were believable and I loved reading it.

Octavia Woodward: 13 years. Somerset

I was hooked by the time I had turned the first page. Anyone who dislikes this book is crazy and doesn't know how to judge books properly.

Emma Jane Chai Forbes: 10 years. Kuwait

I thought it was brilliantly described, stunning, interesting and exciting I could read the book over and over again. One of my favourite characters is the earth-imp because she is original and funny.

Leila Knight: 11 years. London

Keeps you in suspense throughout. Many wonderful characters with memorable messages on brotherhood, friendship, and childhood.

Aurelia Vandamme: 13 years. London

The Dream Dealer is an unusual book and very different from any other that I have read because it is imaginative, creative and some parts are quite scary and sad. So I would recommend it for anyone older than 8 years of age.

Iona Mitchell: 9 years. London

I was full of excitement and dread, all at the same time, at the prospect of finishing the book.

Emily Pickering: 12 years. Oxfordshire

This is a unique story filled with unusual characters - wrinkly old men, dogs, children and I could almost taste the tempting ice cream. From the moment I opened the book, I couldn't put it down.

Nika Webster: 11 years. London

I've recommended this book to countless people, it's a real 'page burner'. The idea behind this story is out of this world and I loved every chapter with its eccentric characters. The Dream Dealer is clever and devious and his partner the Earth Imp brings humour and fun to the plot. I can't wait for a sequel.

Isobel Bond: 11years. Kent

An exciting story that I could not stop reading. I felt like I was right there with Finn and the Dream Dealer. I loved it!

Ben Wilson: 10 years. Gloucestershire

I thought that the Dream Dealer is a very well written book! It's surely one of my favourites! It's full of suspense, you never never know what will happen next… I would definitely describe it as a " Captivating book".

Charlotte d'Arcangelo: 11 years.   London

The Dream Dealer is a great book and nothing like I've read before. Once I'd started the book, I couldn't put it down. I would recommend it to anyone looking for a really good read.

India Martine: 12 years. Kent

The book was fast-paced, exciting, and thrilling. It keeps you asking yourself what is going to happen next.

Andrew McFarlane: 11 years. Georgia, US

I don't read much because I have dyslexia and it's hard work.
I wanted to know what happened next in the Dream Dealer so
I kept reading. I liked the end because it was happy.

Charlotte Lavender: 12 years. Northampton

It was an amazing page-turner. It kept me up late at night,
trying to find out how it ends. I like the whole twist at the
ending... but don't worry, I'm not going to say what it is.
I have just one question: Is there a sequel?

Benjamin Bremner: 11 years. Kuwait

The Dream Dealer rules. Anyone who doesn't like it is unfit
to read anything except non-fiction. I have a hard time telling
what book is my favorite because I read so many, but this one
is high on the list. When my brother read it, he looked like he
was eating an Ice-Dream.

Connett Bremner: 13 years. Kuwait

I couldn't stop reading this book and when I finished it I
started reading it again! My favourite character is Delphi,
because she was the only one nice to Finn.

Arianna Branca: 9 years old. London

It is a book full of imagination and suspense.
Very thrilling and I enjoyed it greatly.

Joshua Smith: 13 years. London

It's the best book I've ever read. I really wish I was
best friends with Delphi.

Abigail Hambidge: 9 years. Oxfordshire

The Dream Dealer

	Page
The Newspaper	1
The Playground	7
The Dream Dealer	11
The New Girl	20
Mixing and Fixing	26
Flake's Visit	31
The Art Lesson	35
The Van	46
The Wig	52
Detentions	58
The English Lesson	61
Ice-Dreams	67
The Answer	75
Guarding the Gates	81
The Experiment	86
Eavesdropping	91

Alf's Dogs	100
The Lucky Break	109
The Photograph	116
The Dinosaur Egg	119
Drink	125
The Birthday	128
Half Twins	136
Magical Sun	141
The Yellow-Eyed Man	147
Mr T. Notices Something	153
The Splinter	159
The Ash Tree	164
Delphi Wakes Up	171
A Dream That Will Last	179
Finn's Money	182
Finn's Dream	185
Immortality	193
Scorcher's Nightmare	198
Time To Move On	204
The Broken Jar	208
Meeting Up	217
May 30th	225
Epilogue to the Yewton Myth	231

The Newspaper

Finn scraped mould off an old piece of cheddar and began making sandwiches for himself and his dad. He glanced round the kitchen, hoping to find something edible. The tins were empty, the crisp packets flat and the only sign of food was a pizza crust left sticking to a pile of plates in the sink.

His father wandered sleepily into the kitchen, his hair sticking up on one side, his shirt half on.

'Good lad,' he said, giving Finn's shoulder a pat. 'Is it school today?'

Hercules, a brown house-mouse, poked his head out of Finn's sleeve and jumped lightly onto the table. He sniffed the scraps of cheese and then, holding a bit between his two paws, nibbled with such speed that his whiskers vibrated. Alf, an old man and friend of Finn's, had rescued Hercules from the mouth of one of his dogs. He had been tiny and hairless and Finn had fed him milk from a fountain pen until he was big enough to eat crumbs and cardboard and chocolate and cheese.

Finn opened the fridge door, which he had plastered with pictures of dogs and insects. He took out a carton of milk and smelled it distrustfully before pouring it into two waiting mugs of tea.

This was home. A home with no magic, or mystery, or mother. Father Christmas had never come down the chimney and left Finn a rustling, bulging stocking. No fairy had bothered to replace his baby-teeth with a silver coin. And no-one had ever suggested to him that there was a god in the sky who would answer his prayers if he tried to be good.

'Tea's ready,' said Finn, tearing a page off yesterday's newspaper to wrap up his sandwich.

His dad snatched up the remaining paper and stuffed it in the already full bin. Finn was suspicious. Why had his dad thrown away the paper and not the crisp packets?

'Seen my bag?' Finn asked, knowing it was hanging behind the bathroom door.

'I'll have a look for it. You'd better not be late for school. Not on the first day of term,' said his father, as he left the kitchen.

Finn rushed to the bin and pulled out the newspaper. There it was: a headline that made his heart thump.

MOTHER FINDS LONG LOST DAUGHTER AFTER 30 YEARS.

He ripped the page out and pushed it in his pocket. He was just throwing the newspaper back in the bin when his father came into the kitchen with his bag.

'What are you doing?' he asked.

'Getting the washing up liquid,' lied Finn.

His dad flung the bag onto the table and turned away.

There was a wretched silence. Finn put Hercules up his sleeve. Dad handed him his bag and muttered,

'There's a pack of lemon sherbets.'

Finn left the house. He hated secrets. They were like black holes. They took all his energy away and made him feel as if he were suffocating. There were so many things he wanted to ask his father, so many things he was not allowed to talk about. So many secrets. He took a deep breath of air.

In the kitchen Dad sighed heavily. With dread he picked the paper out of the bin and opened it. The page he had wanted to hide was of course missing.

'Why do you have to do this to me, Finn?' he thought. 'Why torture me?'

Climbing on a kitchen chair, he reached up into the top cupboard and pulled down a half-empty bottle of whisky. He poured some into his mug of tea and sat down at the table. He took a blunt pencil and began to make a list on the back of an envelope.

Bacon.
Bread.
Milk.
Go to the job centre.
3, 9, 23, 33,47
2, 7, 23, 29, 41
Buy a lottery ticket.

He pushed the list away, his eyes unblinking and lifeless as he drank his tea.

*   *   *

As soon as Finn had turned the corner he pulled the crumpled piece of newspaper out of his pocket and started to read it:

> Mrs Mavis Pratt of Bodington had a fantastic surprise after breakfast on Sunday. Listening to Paul Scott's morning 'Your Music for Me' show, she heard a birthday request for June Pratt. Mavis nearly fainted because June was the name of her daughter who left home 30 years ago to work in America, and had not been heard of since. And today was her long-lost daughter's birthday.
>
> Mavis immediately called Radio Seven. Paul Scott's team tracked down June Pratt and yesterday mother and daughter were reunited. 'It's the happiest day of my life,' said Mavis; June Pratt says this was the 'best birthday present ever.'

'I bet it is,' thought Finn, scrunching up the newspaper and throwing it among the empty packs of cigarettes and plastic bags that littered the street.

Perhaps he should write to the local radio station and ask for a birthday request for Finn Stevens, 12 years old. But would his mother be listening?

As he reached the bus stop he noticed one of the boys from his class. Cal looked at Finn as if he were a piece of spat-out chewing gum. Finn joined the queue and ignored him.

'Hi, Cal,' said another voice.

It was Turk, with a new hairstyle. Green and gelled. A bit like a pterodactyl, thought Finn.

'Where've you spent your holidays, Finn? Ibiza?'

'Going there next holidays,' said Finn, before he could stop himself.

'As if!' smirked Turk.

Cal laughed hard. He'd never been abroad either.

'Did you get to the game on Saturday?' Turk continued, turning his back on Finn.

'No. I'd have killed to see us win,' answered Cal.

He'd had to stay at home to mind his younger brothers. He'd given them every biscuit and crisp in the kitchen to keep them quiet.

'D'you go?'

'No, but I could've. My uncle can always get tickets,' bragged Turk, as he eyed Cal's new trainers.

A bus arrived, drowning out their conversation. Finn pushed his way on and found a seat near the front. He decided not to take Hercules out of his sleeve. The woman next to him looked like one of those types who, when they see a mouse, jump on a chair and scream.

He stared out of the window. The sprawling mass of concrete, tarmac, lights and litter merged into a blur as his thoughts returned, once again, to his mother. Dad had never ever mentioned her. He had made it absolutely clear that he didn't wish Finn to, either. For years Finn had never really questioned it, but now he burned with curiosity. He could think of little else. He wanted to know what she looked like. He wanted to know her name. He wanted to know if she was alive.

'I must have had a mother,' he thought. 'I am going to find her.'

The Playground

F inn was in no hurry to get to school. Walking in front of him were two girls from his class. He watched Bela's hair bounce up and down as she chattered and prattled to Meg as though every word was the most exciting news to have hit the planet. Finn wondered how girls found so much to talk about.

Bela turned and saw him. She whispered something to Meg and they giggled, and quickened their pace. Finn felt the familiar stab of being an outsider. A breeze swept across his face. He stopped and looked up through the rustling branches of the large chestnut tree that grew on the corner of School Lane. Over the holidays the leaves had unfurled, like luminous green fingers on a spread-out hand. They enfolded and held him and he was no longer sure what was him and what was the tree. Time seemed to stop.

He pulled a shrivelled, dull-coloured conker from his pocket and looked at it lying in the palm of his hand. He had kept it since last autumn – it had even survived a turn through the washing machine. What was in this conker? What bit knew how to grow into this huge, beautiful chestnut tree? Could there be some tiny Finn-bit in him that knew how to become fully himself?

The sound of a heavy drum-beat cut through the babble of children's voices. It came from a yellow convertible driven by a woman dressed almost entirely in leopard skin.

'Scorcher's car,' thought Finn, as it zipped past.

'Has to be Scorcher's mum,' said Bela, watching it come to an abrupt stop.

'Why doesn't someone catch that woman and stick her in the zoo?' added Meg. 'My mum's embarrassing but not like that.'

'Your mum's sweet,' said Bela. She looked over Meg's shoulder to see if anyone else interesting was entering the playground. 'Is it true she can't read or…? I just think it's amazing you being the brightest in the class when your mother …' she continued weakly but it was too late. Meg's eyes blazed behind her purple-rimmed glasses and she stormed away.

'What was all that about?' wondered Finn, as he saw Bela gazing desperately after her friend.

As he came near her she turned away and pretended to look in her bag. The shame of being seen with Finn was clearly worse than being seen alone.

'Hi,' said a girl and boy as they pushed past Finn and headed eagerly towards Bela. They were Abi and Jed, the twins with the shiny dark eyes and straight black hair. Finn tried to imagine his mother's hair. Would it be like Abi's or would it stick out in spirals like Bela's?

'You play the saxophone, don't you?' said Abi.

'Yeah,' Bela nodded, unsure as to whether she should be seen talking to anyone in the year below.

'Told you. That's five three to me,' crowed Jed to his twin with whom he ran a daily contest.

'Will you play it for us in break?' asked Abi.

'Everyone says you're brilliant,' Jed added.

'Thanks,' said Bela, looking as if a bit of air had been blown back into her balloon.

'Hi, Scorcher,' she said, catching sight of a tall, confident boy striding in her direction. 'D'you have a good holiday?'

'Went skiing for a month – as you can see,' he said, showing off his sun-tanned face.

'Still on the poverty line?' he called out, as he drew alongside Finn.

'Yeah. I'm still saving.'

'Good. I've got plenty of jobs for you. Maths homework for one,' he added, winking at Abi.

'He's hot,' said Abi, gazing after him. 'I wish he was in our class.'

Finn sat down outside the entrance to Yewton High. The bell had gone for the first lesson but he wanted a few minutes' peace. He undid his trainers and stretched his aching toes. There was no choice, he would have to spend some of his saved money on a bigger pair.

His calculations were interrupted by the sight of Trixie racing across the empty playground. She looked angry and it reminded him of how much he disliked her.

'Always late,' he thought, unaware of how badly she had wanted to be on time.

Finn would never have guessed the reason. Her mother, as usual, had gone out for the evening with her boyfriend and not come home. Trixie had comforted her little sister and taken her to play-school.

'Oh it's you,' she said, looking at Finn with disgust. 'Mr Natural History Channel – what are you studying? Ants?'

'No. Trainers. You've got ketchup on yours.'

'So?' challenged Trixie, staring aggressively at him. Finn opened the cuff of his shirt and Hercules ran obediently up to his elbow and settled down.

'Weirdo!' spat out Trixie, appearing a bit more in control of her day.

'Weirdo, yourself,' muttered Finn to himself.

The Dream Dealer

At the same time, in another town, others were just ending their day.

An attractive man emerged from a basement club with two scantily clad young women. The early summer sun glared down on them and the man hurriedly reached into the pocket of his black leather jacket for his dark glasses. Even in this short time you couldn't fail to notice his eyes. They were an unusual colour, but even more distinct was their laser-like gaze which seemed to pierce whatever they rested on.

'Nice,' he said, admiring a large advertisement.

A well-known actress was wearing pink lace underwear, which somehow suggested you couldn't live without Strawberry Popcorn. The two girls giggled. He put an arm round each of them and they swayed their way down the street. A black Ferrari was parked on the road outside a betting shop. The man's eyes glowed as he disentangled himself from the girls.

He circled the Ferrari, stroking it like a Persian cat. As he placed his hand on one of its curves, his expression suddenly changed from pleasure to irritation. His hand was beginning to age. Wrinkles were appearing like worms crawling across his skin, the colour turning a dirty brown. Quickly, he pulled on a pair of gloves and turned his attention to his companions.

'I've work to do, girls. You'd better run off and get your beauty sleep.'

One girl giggled, the other yawned and together they trotted off on their high heels. The Dream Dealer headed home. There was no time to waste.

A house stood with its blinds closed, looking much like any other. A tabby cat appeared from behind a bin and miaowed plaintively at the Dream Dealer. He kicked the cat with a sickening thud. It flew over the bins and landed, bones rattling, on a parked car.

'No nine lives for you,' he muttered, putting his finger on the bell and holding it there.

A nervous figure came to the door. He was large and round but seemed to take up no more space than a shadow.

'Out of the way, Flake,' said the Dream Dealer pushing past him.

Suitcases and boxes stood packed ready to go.

A large plasma screen, with the picture set on 'pause', displayed a group of armed gangsters on motorbikes being pursued by police cars. Pulling his gloved hands out of his pockets, the Dream Dealer picked up the controls and skilfully killed off two cops.

Now the worm-like wrinkles had begun to crawl up his neck and into his face.

'My medicine, Flake. Hurry!' shouted the Dream Dealer, throwing down the controls and heading for a locked door.

Flake rushed across the room, fumbling with a bunch of keys. After three attempts and some angry growls from the Dream Dealer, Flake succeeded in undoing the lock and they both entered the private room.

Rows of bottles in varying hues lined the walls. Flake identified another key and, holding it in front of him, headed for the safe in the corner of the room. He dragged open the heavy door and pulled out a magnificent rock crystal Jar. Its shimmering surface split the light and, like a prism, sent shafts of rainbow-colours flashing round the room. The Jar pulsated gently in Flake's hands. It felt almost alive.

'Here, B-boss', he stuttered, attaching an oxygen mask to it and handing it to the Dream Dealer.

The inside of the Jar was filled with a swirling, multi-coloured vapour. The Dream Dealer inhaled - deeply. Flake watched as the level of the coloured vapour dropped. Gradually the wrinkles on the

Dream Dealer's neck and face subsided, then faded away altogether. He removed his leather gloves.

'B-better, B-b-boss?' enquired Flake.

'Good man, Flake' answered the Dream Dealer, rewarding his side-kick with a pat. 'Now get the scales.'

Sitting on top of the safe was a little female Earth-imp. Flake couldn't see her, nor could any human. She was visible only to the Dream Dealer. Her skin was not dissimilar to an over-baked potato. Her body continuously changed shape, for it was designed for a place made up of small passages and varying gravitational forces. There was no species on earth that she resembled because she had originated, like the Dream Dealer himself, from not just another part of the planet but another dimension altogether.

Below the earth's crust a whole other world of life and activity exists. Millions of earth-imps, like her, care for the layers of minerals and fossils and clean the tectonic plates. They work, directly, for the sovereign of the planet – Mother Nature, herself.

'Three steps forward and two back,' muttered the Dream Dealer, as he held up the Jar and measured the vapour with an expert eye.

The little Earth-imp scowled and turned her back on him.

'Don't get angry, my darling,' he said. 'Be patient. It's not so long since I found you.'

It was almost ninety years ago that Mother Nature

had sent the little Earth-imp to help the survivors of the Kanto earthquake in Japan.

Whenever the earth is going to shake or stretch or belch or sneeze, as every living thing must do, Mother Nature sends one of her creatures up from the earth's core to the land's surface with a jar of liquid gold. The radiance of this purest of metals lights the area for those who have survived the disaster.

When Kanto was torn apart, the Dream Dealer was there watching. He had once been an earth-imp himself – and when he saw this little one scurrying about, he snatched her up before she could disappear back into a crack in the earth. They had been inseparable ever since.

'It took me over a thousand years to discover how to transform myself from an earth-imp to a human,' said the Dream Dealer. 'And I had no-one to help me. You have a huge advantage. You have me. You have my equipment. You have my knowledge of what I have lived through, of what I've had to do. It won't be long, my little one. Trust me.'

The little Earth-imp climbed up the Dream Dealer's arm and gently scratched his face. She never tired of hearing his stories of how he became a human, or rather so nearly fully human.

At that moment Flake, annoyingly, returned with a large metal weighing machine which he carefully placed on a table. The little Earth-imp's body contorted with rage and she stretched out and pinched him on the cheek. He yelped and looked dolefully at his boss.

'Keep going,' ordered the Dream Dealer.

Flake rubbed his cheek and set off, baffled but obedient, to fetch a small wooden box from the safe.

This box had a picture of a Dodo intricately carved on its lid. The Dream Dealer took out a fluffy grey feather which had once belonged to the last Dodo in existence. Carefully he rested it on one side of the scales, moving his hands away slowly so that it did not blow off.

The little Earth-imp had climbed onto a shelf. She began peering at the words engraved on the bottles.

AHMED, 13 YEARS. FOOTBALLER
SAM, 18 YEARS. INVENTOR
LILAC, 16 YEARS. POET

She avoided Flake's hand as he reached for two of the bottles. He carried them over to the Dream Dealer who placed the first one on the scales, opposite the grey Dodo feather. The scales sunk under its weight and the Dream Dealer tried the second bottle but it was also too heavy.

'Another one, Flake. Hurry up. No time to waste.'

Flake brought over a handful of bottles and the Dream Dealer chose the one labelled: VERA, 15 YEARS. SINGER. He placed it on the scales and waited. The scales balanced perfectly. At last.

'Aha! A little beauty.'

With great care the Dream Dealer placed a tube from the bottle into the rock crystal Jar observing the magenta vapour as it flowed from one to the other.

'Chuck this bottle, Flake. If we get her again she'll go directly into my Jar.'

He was proud of his system of soul sorting.

'B-but what makes one b-bottle light enough to b-b-balance and another one n-not?' asked Flake.

'Your guess is as good as mine – which isn't often the case, is it?'

'Talent, is it B-b-b...?'

'All I know is that some souls are as light as the feather and are perfect for my purpose and some are heavy and they are useless,' interrupted the Dream Dealer impatiently.

He was thinking of all the years he had wasted, until he discovered that only breathing in perfect souls could keep him human. Before that, he had mixed the good and the bad in his Jar but this had greatly weakened the effect of his precious potion. It was a painstaking process but at least the system worked.

Two hours later the floor lay littered with discarded bottles. Flake had noticed that whenever he broke a bottle the vapour escaped, like a coloured comet, and whistled out through the window. He watched but never questioned where it went.

'Tidy those up ready for next time, Flake,' said

the Dream Dealer wearily picking up the last un-weighed bottle. It was labelled: KIT, 12 YEARS. ---.

He put it on the scales and watched as they remained perfectly still. The little grey feather one side and the bottle with golden vapour exactly balancing it on the other.

'I don't understand, B-boss. It doesn't say what he was g-g-good at?' said Flake.

'It seems nothing in particular,' replied the Dream Dealer, continuing to stare at the bottle. 'Golden vapour is rare, very rare.'

'I don't g-get it ....'

'It's his soul, Flake. Old and refined. Pure as poetry. Light as air. Not a stain to weigh it down.'

The Dream Dealer removed the feather. Still the scales didn't move.

'That is a truly perfect soul.'

'B-b-but who was Kit?'

'Probably a nobody,' mused the Dream Dealer.

Over the centuries of weighing human souls he had never found one famous person whose soul-vapour was gold – not an artist, not a hero, not a saint. Those golden few had seemed to him ordinary, at one with themselves, at one with life, and extraordinarily hard to lure into his trap.

'I don't g-get it...'

'Nor are you meant to,' snapped the Dream Dealer. 'You take care of clearing all this up and I'll take care of you, right?'

Flake nodded as he began stacking the empty bottles back on the shelf.

Those strange eyes glinting, the Dream Dealer siphoned off the vapour from the bottle labelled 'Kit' and watched as the swirls of gold sank to the bottom of the Jar, causing the level of the coloured vapour to rise and rise.

'Excellent. If I could find just one more like him...   Load the Van, Flake. Be ready to go.'

The New Girl

F inn opened the cuff of his jersey and shook his arm. Mouse droppings fell onto the tarmac.

'Yuk!' said Bela.

'What d'you think of that new girl. Delphi?' asked Trixie, turning her back on Finn. 'Comes from Australia.'

'She's pretty. Cool clothes and…'

Bela stopped abruptly and began fiddling with the new ring in her belly button. Delphi had come into the playground. Finn hardly dared look up. She seemed to be walking in his direction.

'Hi,' she said. 'No-one told me your name.'

Finn looked at her smiling, open face. But as he said his name, Trixie stepped between them, eyed him as if he were vomit, and said to Delphi,

'I'd better warn you, it's no good hanging out with Finn.'

'Not if you want to be popular,' explained Bela.

Finn blinked and looked down at Hercules.

'Why? What's wrong with him?' Delphi asked, looking straight at Trixie.

Trixie turned to a group of boys.

'What would you say was wrong with Finn?'

'He's okay,' answered Scorcher. 'Just a bit of a loser.'

Finn walked slowly away.

'Dresses from the charity shop,' said Turk.

'Walks around with a *mouse*,' scoffed Cal.

'At least it gives him someone to talk to,' joined in Meg, glancing admiringly at Delphi.

'Tells awful lies,' said Bela, not wanting to be left out.

Finn didn't hear anymore.

*   *   *

'I take it he's not your best friend,' said Delphi, staring after Finn.

'No way,' sneered Trixie. 'Hey, you don't speak at all like they do on *Neighbours*.'

Delphi laughed and so did the kids.

'For a start I'm not *Oz-stry-le-an*. My step-dad is.'

'You just said the word 'step-dad' like an aussie,' observed Bela, once again showing Delphi her belly-button ring.

'Cool!' exclaimed Delphi. 'My mum would kill me if I did that. What did yours say when she saw?'

'Never noticed,' answered Bela bitterly. 'She doesn't care what I do.'

'Let's have a kick,' said Cal, floating his football down one arm, spinning it on his finger and then catching it on his foot.

'Wow!' said Delphi. 'Do that again.'

Cal picked up the ball ready to begin the trick again but Turk grabbed it and ran.

'Come on. Let's have a game,' he shouted over his shoulder.

Cal, Scorcher and a group of others raced after him.

'Shall we watch them?' said Trixie.

'I'll see you guys later,' answered Delphi.

Trixie, Bela and Meg stared after her.

*　　*　　*

Delphi walked over to where Finn was studying something in the ivy on the wall.

'What is it?' she asked.

Finn jumped as if he had been caught doing something wrong.

'A blackbird's nest. They've hatched. There's four.'

'I didn't know birds made nests in towns,' said Delphi.

'Course they do,' chuckled Finn. 'They're not exactly going to pack their bags and go to the country to have babies.' They giggled together.

Birds with suitcases.

'I've got a couple of worms. D'you want to give one?' asked Finn.

'No way!' said Delphi.

Finn took out a small pink worm. He parted the ivy with one hand, revealing a neat nest with what appeared to be four little bags of skin. He touched one and it immediately stretched out a long, wobbly neck at the end of which was a huge, open, yellow beak. Finn popped the worm in to it and as it closed, three more beaks opened so wide that Delphi thought they were going to dislocate their jaws.

'I've never seen anything like it in my life,' she gasped. 'Let's have a go.'

Without hesitation Delphi picked out the other worm and dangled it over the straining mouths. One of the yellow beaks closed on the worm and Delphi laughed with excitement.

'Have you shown anyone else?' she asked.

'No way. Do you want to hold Hercules?'

Finn held out his mouse and Delphi nervously took him.

'Help, it tickles,' she squealed. 'Take him back before he pees on me.'

'Hercules likes you,' Finn said, rescuing the mouse.

'How d'you know?'

'He didn't bite.'

'Great!' said Delphi. 'I've only got a goldfish. We had a dog but we had to leave him behind.'

'I'm saving for a puppy,' said Finn.

'Why don't you go to a dog's home. You'd get one free.'

'I want a Sheltie. And I want it small– straight from its mum.'

'Won't your mum and dad buy you one?'

For a moment Finn hesitated but decided it was too complicated to tell her the truth.

'Dad's job doesn't pay much. But I haven't got to pay the full amount. I'm going to have the runt.'

'What's a runt?' asked Delphi.

'The one nobody wants,' answered Finn pulling an old wallet from his pocket. 'I've got to save 60 quid. Look, I've got 47.'

Delphi looked around nervously.

'You're crazy bringing it to school. You'll get it stolen.'

'It's safer here than at home.'

'Why? Is your dad a burglar?' joked Delphi.

'Course not,' he answered sharply and then catching Delphi's mood he giggled with her. 'D'you ever go surfing?'

'Every weekend.'

'Wow! I want to surf. Whatever made you come back?'

'My mum got very unhappy.'

'Why?'

Delphi shrugged.

'Anyway, one day my step-dad said he'd got a job

in England and we were going to look for treasure or something.'

'Let me know if I can help,' said Finn.

'Wish you could. I'm fed up with moving schools. This is the third one I've been to in Yewton,' said Delphi. 'Promise not to tell anyone about this.'

'Course not. And same with what I've told you,' said Finn.

For a while neither spoke but each understood the other.

Mixing and Fixing

T**he Dream Dealer had arrived in Yewton. For the past couple of weeks Flake had been blundering around, hammering shelves, fixing locks and generally irritating the Dream Dealer. Now the new flat was ready for action and Flake, thank heaven, was out of it, researching schools in the town.

The Dream Dealer had closed the curtains and was engrossed in a game of internet poker. He had been dealt a Queen and a Seven.

'What do you think, little one? Shall I go for it or fold?'

The little Earth-imp had her nose pressed to the computer screen. She was looking at the other players' cards. She turned to the Dream Dealer and screwed up her face.

'Okay. I'll fold. We've won a thousand. That will do for today.'

The Dream Dealer flicked off the computer and began to pace up and down the room.

'I'm sick of hanging round schools, searching for souls,' he snarled. 'Sick of this struggle to stay human. Sick of being followed around by that fool, Flake.'

The Earth-imp leapt off the table and lumbered across the floor in an imitation of Flake. She pretended to trip on an imaginary object, landing on her back with her legs in the air. She sat up laboriously and stared at the Dream Dealer with a look of Flake-like adoration, her pupils dilated and her mouth hanging open. The Dream Dealer laughed.

Flake appeared through the door with a half-eaten doughnut in one hand and carrying a pad of paper in the other. He gazed questioningly at his boss.

'How was this morning's school?' barked the Dream Dealer.

'Hard to say, B-boss. No music rooms, no sport, nnnno ...'

'...discipline? No structure? How can I see the kids' potential? Forget it.'

The Dream Dealer grabbed the list of schools from Flake and quickly marked a large X by the names of three.

'Check 'em out, Flake. But first let's fix the ice-creams.'

Over the centuries, the Dream Dealer had conjured up many an imaginative ploy to procure the precious vapour for his Jar. But his current use of ice-creams had proved the most successful of all. This was helped by the fact that today's teenagers were more susceptible to his charms than ever before.

Flake followed the Dream Dealer into the room that was always kept locked, unaware of the little Earth-imp sitting on the end of his boss's shoe. Sunlight was shining onto a large, jagged crystal especially placed on the windowsill. The Earth-imp climbed onto a chair and studied it. The Dream Dealer picked up the crystal. Large drops of converted sunshine fell from it into a glass bowl, where they lay like a liquid rainbow.

'Moonbeam, darling,' whispered the Dream Dealer to the little Earth-imp. 'Thanks, love,' he added, taking a small tube from her as she struggled towards him.

Flake looked across at the Dream Dealer, surprised that he was being called 'love'. He continued sorting a collection of strangely shaped ice-cream cones. Each had been carefully baked and decorated. He put a piece in his mouth and nodded with satisfaction.

'Here, Flake. I need you to stir,' ordered the Dream Dealer, as he poured his special concoction into a huge tub.

He squeezed some opal drops into the mixture and a fine mist rose out of it.

'Quick. Stir it in. Stir it in.'

Flake hurried to the tub and grasping the long wooden spoon with both hands, pushed it in circles through the thick, coloured mixture. Tiny bubbles flew out and floated round the room.

'This is what kids need these days – poor things. All that stress and strain. They're hardly allowed to be kids anymore. Don't you agree, Flake?'

'This makes them feel b-better, right?' said Flake, his face becoming quite pink and hot from stirring.

'Course. Of course. Even the smell of it gives a sense of well-being. Now where are the Habit Granules?' he added, waving the clouds of bubbles away so he could see.

'B-by the cones, B-boss.'

'Good man. You're doing a great job.'

A proud smile spread across Flake's red face as he gazed at the Dream Dealer. The spoon had risen higher and higher in the mixture. Suddenly it flicked a large splodge straight on to the Dream Dealer's immaculate leather coat.

'You great globbering fool,' he shrieked, stamping as hard as he could on Flake's foot.

Flake's face crumpled in pain. The little Earth-imp puffed-up into a ball and bounced across the floor, exploding with laughter. The Dream Dealer wiped the mixture off his jacket and shook a generous portion of Habit Granules into the mixture.

'Finish this job, moron. Then get over and see that school.'

*   *   *

Flake nodded, not daring to look up until he heard the door slam. Miserably, he poured the mixture into the ice-cream-making machine and switched it on. He had lost count of how many years he had toured from school to school in town after town. Last month Brimsfield, this month Yewton. He had lost most memories of his life before the Dream Dealer. He had lost ...he couldn't remember what he had lost.

He opened the machine and helped himself to a large spoonful of the creamy mixture. It was better not to think. Better not to feel. Better to be happy. After all, who doesn't want to be happy?

Flake's Visit

Flake whistled as he walked across the empty playground of Yewton High School. He swung a toolbox hoping people would think he was a plumber. Hearing the sound of piano scales and the rasping of a violin, he decided he would start his search with the music block. A teacher stopped him in the passage.

'Can I help you?' she asked.

'Just seeing to a l-leaking radiator, thanks,' answered Flake, pointing towards the sound of instruments and hurrying away.

He knelt by a radiator outside the practice rooms and opened his toolbox. Someone was playing the saxophone. He peered through the glass and caught sight of Bela, her curly hair bouncing with the beat. A younger boy was watching her with obvious admiration. He had shiny dark eyes. Then a girl with identical shiny dark eyes walked down the passage, carrying a violin case with the name Abi written on it. His face screwed up in confusion. Life was a continual mystery to Flake.

He picked up a hammer and knocked it a few times on the radiator, causing some of the paint to fall off. Flustered, he looked up and there, unless his eyes were playing tricks, was a boy and girl version of the same person. He put his hands over his face hoping that, if he gave himself a bit of time, things would return to normal.

But when he looked again, they were still there and what's more they were arguing with each other.

'Twins! That's it,' thought Flake with relief. 'TWINS! The Boss would be very pleased. Very pleased indeed. He was always looking for twins.'

Feeling quite cheerful he set off to see what else he could discover. Just then lessons ended and Flake found himself caught up in a wave of children, talking, pushing, shoving, and swarming round him. When the flood subsided Flake discovered he had been swept into another part of the building and deposited outside the Art Room. His eyes lit up. He liked painting. He stood by the door hoping his large frame was invisible and waiting for the right moment to enter without being noticed.

The bell had gone for the next lesson but there was no sign of children hurrying to the art class. Eventually a solitary boy wandered towards Flake.

He was carrying something small and furry in one hand. The boy looked through the glass window of the art room and, when he saw nobody else had yet arrived, he sat down with his back against the wall, put the mouse up his sleeve and took a piece of paper and a pen out of his pocket.

* * *

Finn hadn't noticed Flake. His mind was on other things. He had spent the first weeks of term thinking and thinking of a way to find out if his mother was alive. He had overheard Trixie mention that there was a place where everybody's births, marriages and deaths were recorded. He had typed BIRTHS, MARRIAGES, DEATHS into the search engine on the school computer and tried to trace his family. That soon proved impossible because he didn't know his mother's name or the date when his parents were married. And even when he typed his own name into the Search box, it came up with 'Are you sure you mean Finn Stevens. 0 matches for this name.' He decided to write a letter instead. The only problem was how to start. He chewed the end of his pen and wrote;

> Dear I dont know your name
> I want to find out the name of my mum.
> My father is called Mike Stevens and he

probly married my mum about 12 years
ago. Can you help. From Finn Stevens

He had just completed it when he heard the sound of voices coming closer. He stood up and vaguely noticed a large figure slipping into the art room. The figure then settled down by a radiator, opened his toolbox and appeared to be working busily.

The Art Lesson

A rt had to be the most boring lesson in Finn's week. He couldn't see the point of it. He sometimes thought it would be fun to have a camera. But to spend an hour producing an unrecognisable tangle of lines that were meant to be a vase with a flower sticking out of it, seemed a complete waste of time. Added to which the art teacher was more of a joke than an inspiration.

Mr Turpentine was tall and thin and always wore an immaculately clean grey artist's smock. His hair was tied neatly in a ponytail and he was never without his black beret, set at an artistic angle on his head.

'You're late. You're all late. Hurry up and settle down. Stop talking. Over here everybody…' shouted the frantic art teacher.

Neither Finn nor anyone else paid the faintest bit of attention. Mr Turpentine put a silver policeman's whistle up to his mouth and let out a series of shrill blasts. The children briefly stopped chattering. He seized the moment of silence.

'Finn, come here. You are going to be the model.'

'But I've been the model every week since the beginning of term,' protested Finn.

'That's because you can't draw. Now sit here and put that mouse away.'

'I have, Sir.'

'You have not. I can see it up your sleeve.'

'He's asleep.'

'Gross,' said Cal. 'It poos up his sleeve.'

Mr Turpentine bustled busily from one side of the room to the other, carrying pots of paints, dropping brushes and shouting out orders to which nobody listened. Cal had drawn two posts on the board and he and Turk were chucking rubbers at it to see who could score the most goals. Meg had made herself comfortable in a corner and was reading 'Pride and Prejudice'. Bela was carefully applying blue polish to her nails.

'What d'you think you're doing?' roared Mr Turpentine, as he staggered past trying to balance a huge stash of paper.

'Painting, Sir,' answered Bela, without looking up.

Mr T. sighed dramatically as he dropped the paper in a pile on the floor, followed by a balletic gesture with his arms that was meant to indicate they should all take a sheet and start work.

'Have you ever met such a rubbish teacher?' said Trixie, collecting a piece of paper and some paints and giving them to Delphi.

Delphi giggled.

'Watch this,' said Trixie, turning to the teacher.

'Mr Turpentine? Sir?' she questioned in her politest voice. 'You know you teach art?'

'Obviously,' he answered.

'Can you actually paint?'

'Well. Yes. I mean…'

'Can we see,' she continued ruthlessly. 'Do a painting for us now.'

'Don't be cheeky. I'm teaching, you're learning,' he spluttered.

'I don't think he can,' commented Trixie.

Mr Turpentine pulled himself up to his full height and exclaimed,

'Now listen here. I was the youngest student ever at the Central College of Art. I was your age. I was a child prodigy. I was… I was…'

'So what exactly happened, Sir?' interrupted Turk.

Flake was staring at Mr Turpentine as if something was stirring in the porridge of his mind. It was as if he vaguely recognised him yet couldn't remember from where or when.

'…and who are you. I said WHO ARE YOU?'

The voice was getting louder, getting nearer. Suddenly Flake realised Mr Turpentine was addressing him.

'The p-plumber. There's an air l-lock....Sir,' stuttered Flake, loosening the valve at the side of the radiator.

It flew off and a jet of water spurted straight into Mr Turpentine's face. While he spluttered and coughed, the children revelled in the entertainment. Flake trundled across the room to retrieve the valve. He managed to replace it and shutting his toolbox, he hurried from the room.

'Wait! Wait! I want to talk to you. Come back...' cried the dripping Mr Turpentine.

Scorcher had settled himself in front of Finn with a large sheet of paper and some paints. Finn could never understand how Scorcher was able, by filling in a few blocks of colour, to produce a picture which actually resembled a figure sitting on a chair. A few other children gathered round Finn and also began to paint. Mr Turpentine wandered round the room criticising the children's work.

'And what's that meant to be?' he said to Turk.

'An arm, Sir.'

'Arms don't grow out of people's ears,' pronounced Mr T. tapping the paper with his finger. 'You should eat more fish. It's good for the brain cells.'

Mr Turpentine moved away before turning to say, 'And in your case I recommend a whale.'

Turks face burned.

'Sir,' said Meg. 'A whale's not a fish, it's a mam...'

Mr Turpentine whipped round and glared at

her painting.

'And you Miss Clever-clogs, need to eat carrots – are you blind? How is your hair attached to your head?'

He held up her hair, nearly causing her glasses to fall off.

'Ow! Roots, Sir,' she squealed.

'Correct,' he said, letting go of her hair. 'This looks like a bowl of spaghetti.'

Meg screwed up her piece of paper and threw it on the floor.

The children whooped gleefully as they set about imitating Mr Turpentine.

'What's that meant to be? Finn or a toilet brush?'

'Same thing.'

'What have we here? A caterpillar?'

'It's really creepy. It looks like Finn.'

'Can't we draw someone else.'

'He's got a spot on his nose.'

'His hair's manky.'

'He stinks.'

'He's ugly.'

Finn concentrated on counting the dirty marks on the floor. It didn't help. He could hear every word they were saying.

Mr Turpentine was circling the children trying to restore some order. He stood on a chair and shouted,

'Get back to your places and PAINT FINN.'

Cal heard the last two words and decided to obey.

He grabbed a couple of pots of paint and strode towards Finn.

'Come on everyone.'

He threw the paint straight at Finn. Some of it went in his eyes and stung. He jumped up but he was surrounded by all the children throwing paint, chucking screwed-up bits of paper and poking him with their brushes. He couldn't escape. Delphi frantically tried to pull the children away but they shook her off.

Finally, Mr Turpentine's whistle penetrated the madness and the children gradually seemed to remember where they were and wandered back to their places. Finn was left curled up on the floor with barely a part of him not covered in paint.

Delphi knelt beside him and asked if he was all right. Of course he wasn't all right but at least she still wanted to talk him. He stood up and walked out of the room.

* * *

Mr Turpentine blew one final useless peep from his whistle as he watched Finn go.

Delphi turned on the kids, her eyes flashing, her hands shaking with rage.

'You're the nastiest… sickest…vilest bunch of psychos I've ever, ever, ever met. I'd like to pour paint in your eyes and see how you like it. What's Finn done anyway? Why can't you leave him alone? I hate this school…I hate this country…I hate all of you…'

Delphi put her hands over her face and sobbed.

The children shuffled uncomfortably, not looking at one another.

Scorcher, who had watched the incident from the far side of the room, walked over to Delphi. He stood there, awkwardly, holding his painting and saying nothing.

Mr Turpentine was lost. He was shocked at what had taken place and shocked by his own inability to do anything. His mind felt paralysed. He stared into the distance and wished as hard as he could that it would all go away. His body began to sway and a strange humming noise came from him, like a distant motorbike.

Delphi uncovered her eyes and gazed at him incredulously. Was he a teacher or was he some idiot character from a kid's cartoon?

Soon all the children's attention was on Mr Turpentine, Finn conveniently pushed from their minds.

Cal began humming and swaying in time with the teacher. As he did so, he glanced at Turk. Turk snorted and, instantly, the kids exploded into giggles.

It had worked. Mr Turpentine opened his eyes. He didn't know what had happened but clearly everything was in order again. Only Delphi was glaring at him as though he were standing there in pyjamas.

'Do something!' she shouted.

'Do something,' he repeated weakly, hoping that by some miracle he would.

Why did those words fill him with panic? It was like being asked to run when his feet had pins and needles. He couldn't. He couldn't do anything. What had happened? Why had he become like this? Why did thinking give his brain pins and needles?

'You're meant to be the teacher, for heaven's sake,' continued Delphi.

'Indeed, indeed – and this is an art class,' exhaled Mr Turpentine, grasping onto something familiar. 'Now get back to your places, all of you. Get on with your paintings while I think of a suitable punishment.'

The children's laughter subsided as they slowly picked up their bits of paper and flattened out the creases. They daubed paint on them aimlessly and watched the clock, hoping the lesson would end before Mr Turpentine came up with an idea.

'Got it!' he cried triumphantly. 'You will learn the names of artists. Get in a line. Hurry up.'

The children dropped their paintings on the floor and, deliberately bumping into each other, shuffled into an untidy row.

'Say after me: Bacon, Brueghel, Canaletto,' sang out Mr T., waving his arms like the conductor of an orchestra.

'Bacon, Brueghel, Canaletto,' parroted the class.

'Sausage, Bagel, Cannelloni,' muttered Turk. Cal and Tiffy started giggling.

'You'll stay in during lunch. Concentrate!' shouted Mr T. 'Degas, Durer, Goya, Gauguin, Lely, Lippi, Monet, Manet, Poussin, Picasso, Renoir, Rembrandt, Titian, Tintoretto…'

'What about Turpentine?' interrupted Trixie, instinctively knowing what effect the mention of his name would have.

She was right. It was as if she had pushed a stick into the spokes of a revolving bicycle wheel. He stopped. His eyes went out of focus as he stared into an imaginary copy of the Dictionary of Art and Artists. There was his name, B. Turpentine following straight on from J. M. W. Turner. Now the kids had to make sure he didn't start again.

'Look, Mr Turpentine! What d'you think of Scorcher's painting?' called Tiffy, dragging Scorcher over to the teacher.

In a few bold lines Scorcher had captured not just Finn's features but his expression of impatience. Mr Turpentine was impressed. So much so that he forgot about being a famous artist and failed even to hear the bell for lunch.

'Well. Well. Look what we have here? A fine likeness. A very fine likeness. Similar style to me. Good work, Scorcher.'

'Wow!' said Meg, pulling Tiffy towards the door. 'It's brilliant.'

'Brilliant, Scorcher,' echoed the other kids, also making a swift exit.

'Could have had a bit more shading down the left side,' suggested Mr T., a hint of jealousy beginning to creep into his enthusiasm.

Delphi took the picture from Scorcher's hand.

'It's awesome,' she said. 'Can I have it?'

'Sure. D'you really want it?' Scorcher's cheeks pinkened.

Trixie's face distorted as she sneered sarcastically,

'Oh Scorcher. You're so brilliant. Won't you give me that sad little picture. I've always wanted a creepy poster of Finn for my room.'

Delphi glared after Trixie as she strode from the room.

'Hey, Trixie where are you going? Where have you all gone? I haven't said you can go. Come back ...'

Mr T. stared around the emptying room. Only Scorcher and Delphi were left. What had happened? Why did the dots in his life never seem to join up?

'Delphi, come with me to lunch,' said Scorcher.

'Okay. But first I'm going to find Finn. Maybe he wants to come too.'

*   *   *

But Finn didn't go to lunch. He struggled to wash the paint off himself and then hid in the far corner of the playground eating a stale sandwich with a stream of questions pouring through his head: Why didn't they like him? Why couldn't he have been born someone else? Why couldn't they accept him as he was? - Where was the letter he had written?

The thought of the letter cheered him up. He addressed the envelope and then searched his pocket for the unused first class stamp he had found in the rubbish basket. It had no glue on it. He pulled the wrapper off a toffee that Delphi had given him and gave it a good lick. When it was sticky, he rubbed it on the back of the stamp and stuck the stamp firmly on the envelope.

That felt good, it helped him forget that horrible art lesson. He scrambled onto the top of the wall. He could see the letterbox at the end of the street. His stomach tightened. He was excited. At last he was doing something about finding his mother.

The Van

T'he Dream Dealer was walking round a newly painted ice-cream van.

'Nice work, Flake,' he said, admiring the swirling, psychedelic shapes of tempting looking ice lollies and ice-creams. 'Quite fancy one myself.'

Flake sighed contentedly. Happiness for him was praise from his boss.

'Close your eyes, B-boss,' he said, reaching up to the sign that read ICE-CREAMS.

The Dream Dealer blinked and caught Flake changing the C to a D.

'ICE-DREAMS! Very good, very good.'

'D'you like the p-pink wheels?'

'Yes, yes, yes. It's all good now let's get on with the real work. How far is that school from here?'

'Not too far,' answered Flake, realising his moment was over.

He opened the passenger door. The Dream Dealer settled himself into the leather-lined seats and winked at the little Earth-imp who was hanging from the mirror pretending to be a car mascot.

'Bbbbbelt on, B-boss,' said Flake.

He turned on the Sat Nav and fed in Yewton High School. As they drove off, the Dream Dealer pressed a button; a tinkling, tantalising tune cut through the relentless drone of traffic. Grown-ups and children looked up and some even smiled and waved.

'Nice making people happy, isn't it, Flake? It's an art I specialise in. Did you know I got a top degree in psychology? Did you know that?'

'*Next left,*' interrupted the lady on the Sat Nav.

Flake turned left.

'But I've got more than a degree,' continued the Dream Dealer. 'I've got an instinct. I tell you something, Flake. I know more about human beings than they know about themselves.'

'*You are now in the vicinity of your destination,*' interrupted the Sat Nav lady once again.

'Have an Ice-Dream, Flake. A small one,' said the Dream Dealer, glancing at his heavy gold watch. 'And then serve some regular ice-creams. I'm going to relax.'

Flake parked the Van in the shade of the trees not far from the gates of the school. He hadn't been listening to the Dream Dealer's stories. He had been thinking about the art teacher. He'd said he'd been a child prodigy. Flake had once heard that word. When he was a boy, his friend Ben had been called a prodigy. They used to paint together…

Flake helped himself greedily to a small Mystic Bean. He was soon enveloped in a bubble of bliss and any memories of when he was a boy faded from his mind. He opened up the counter and played the tinselly tune a few times. A mother with children and a couple of builders came by and bought ice-creams.

*　　*　　*

The Dream Dealer settled himself in his special compartment in the back of the Van. He lit a cigar and started browsing on the computer for things to buy. As he was typing in the number of his credit card, two small bumps appeared on his head. The little Earth-imp, who had followed him in, began jumping up and down and pointing at his head. The Dream Dealer growled in exasperation as he pulled his crystal Jar out from a panel under the computer, fixed the mask to it and hurriedly breathed in. The level of coloured vapour in the Jar fell. At the same time the bumps on his head shrank and then disappeared.

'It's tedious. Very tedious. But the end is in sight,' he said, holding up the Jar and studying the remaining space between the misty contents and a delicately engraved '∞' – the symbol of infinity.

His final goal was to get the vapour in the Jar up to the infinity level. Then he could be both fully human and ageless. Those few centimetres were all that stood between his present form and immortality.

'Nearly there, nearly there.'

The little Earth-imp stroked the Dream Dealer's head where the bumps had been and nuzzled up against him.

Suddenly from the corner of his eye, the Dream Dealer noticed a child on the top of the school wall. He jumped out of the Van and, like a hovering hawk, remained absolutely still, pinning Finn on the end of his gaze. As Finn jumped off the wall and came towards the Van, the Dream Dealer stepped out of the shadows and, noticing the letter, said in his most helpful voice,

'Hurry. You'll miss the post.'

Sure enough Finn had seen the red van as it drew up by the box. The postman was already tipping the letters into his grey bag. He started to run, his face creased by anxiety.

'Wait! Wait!' he shouted but the postman had thrown the sack into the van and was climbing back into his seat.

A head-splitting wolf-whistle pierced the air. The postman got out and looked around. This gave Finn the extra seconds he needed. He sprinted the last 50 metres and handed the postman the letter.

'Great!' whispered Finn breathlessly to himself.

'That whistle saved me.'

'Good timing. It's your lucky day,' said the postman, closing the van door.

Finn approached the Ice-cream Van but, instead of thanking the Dream Dealer, he stood, as if paralysed.

'Hope your wish comes true,' smiled the Dream Dealer, breaking the spell. Finn focused on the ground and tried to walk away. In a second the Dream Dealer leapt between Finn and the school.

'Saving up your pocket money?'

Finn was silent.

'What are you saving up for?'

'Dog.' Finn answered in a small voice.

'Aha! Flake, do we have any puppy dreams?'

'Yes, Bbbboss, only five pppp –.'

Finn looked at the large stuttering figure standing behind the counter in the Van and then he noticed the sign ICE-DREAMS.

'£5 for a puppy dream. Special offer,' persisted the Dream Dealer.

'I want a real live dog. I don't want a dream.'

'A man is half a man without a dream. Let me help you choose.'

'How can you give me my dream? It already belongs to me,' argued Finn.

'Relax. Relax,' cajoled the Dream Dealer, circling Finn, as if scanning him for clues. 'What is your desire? To be accepted? To be special? To belong to…?'

'None of your business.'

'It is very much my business. I specialise in dreams. Isn't that right, Flake?'

'Right, B-boss.'

Finn tried to walk round the Dream Dealer but once again found his way blocked.

'You're an honest fellow. Integrity's the word that comes to mind.'

'Wrong,' snubbed Finn. 'I'm a liar.'

The Dream Dealer was surprised to hear the boy boasting about something he was probably ashamed about. The boy didn't like him – that was a good sign.

'You're the one who's wrong,' argued the Dream Dealer good-humouredly. 'Liars don't say they are liars.'

Finn dodged past the Dream Dealer and ran back to the school.

'Interesting one. A little research, Flake. Okay?'

The Wig

'**L**iars don't say they are liars.'

The words repeated themselves over and again in Finn's head. As the distance between him and the stranger increased he remembered the Dream Dealer's whistle, how it had enabled him to catch the post. He felt confused. Who was this man? What were Ice-Dreams?

'You're wanted in the detention room,' said a bossy little girl from the year below. 'Someone saw you climbing the wall.'

'Pretend you haven't seen me,' said Finn, knowing he was asking the impossible.

'Sorry. I'm just doing what I'm told.'

Finn decided he might as well get it over now, so he set off towards the staff room. In the distance he saw Delphi. She was chatting to Scorcher. Finn's stomach dropped. How could he compete? Scorcher had everything: he was good looking, he was popular, he had money and he could draw. She obviously fancied Scorcher. She wouldn't waste her time with him again.

*   *   *

'Okay, I'll go out with you,' Delphi was saying, as she offered Scorcher one of her crisps.

'And will you stop being so friendly with Finn,' asked Scorcher confidently.

'No. I like him.'

'Why?' said Scorcher with a surge of annoyance. 'What's so special about him?'

'Nothing's special. It's just easy, that's all.'

Scorcher wasn't going to change her mind, so he pulled a silver pen out of his pocket and handed it to her.

'Here, have this. It's a pen with a camera and a microphone and a radio.'

'Wicked. Can I really have it?'

Scorcher leant over and showed her how to work the radio.

Trixie came running across the playground followed by the rest of the gang. She was waving something in her hand.

'Scorcher! Scorcher! Look what we've …'

She stopped mid-sentence when she saw Scorcher leaning over Delphi.

'Ooh sorry. Are we disturbing the lovebirds? Tweet! Tweet!'

Scorcher ignored her taunt.

'What's that?' he said, looking at a familiar beret with a wig attached to it. 'I don't believe it. Turps wears a wig!'

'D'oh!' said Turk, who had said exactly the same thing a few minutes earlier.

'How did you get it?' asked Scorcher.

Bela, Cal, Turk and Meg, all spoke at once. Mr Turpentine had been sitting in the sun outside the art room. Trixie had leant out of the window and tied a piece of string around the end of his ponytail. The idea was to give it a tug and see if she could get out of the room before he had time to see who had pulled his hair. All had gone to plan except that, as Trixie ran from the room, she noticed Mr Turpentine's hat and hair were attached to the end of the string.

Cal put the hat and wig on his head. Turk grabbed it and did an imitation of Mr Turpentine flapping his arms. Through the laughter, only Bela heard the familiar sound of Mr T.'s whistle.

'He's coming! Quick! Turps is coming!'

Turk whipped off the wig and pushed it into Trixie's hands. Trixie held it behind her back as Mr Turpentine staggered towards them, his bald head glinting.

'Sir? Where's your hair?' asked Trixie in her politest voice.

'Don't be facetious,' spluttered Mr Turpentine, his voice an octave higher than usual.

'*Fa See* what?' said Cal.

'You look really cool, Sir,' said Bela.

'You could tattoo your head,' chimed in Scorcher.

Delphi nodded, overcome by giggles.

'You can get one of the Mona Lisa,' suggested Meg.

'Where is my hat? Who has taken my hat?' shouted Mr Turpentine.

'I think I saw Finn with it, didn't you Turk?' said Cal.

'Yeah. He was just here.'

'Nonsense. I know exactly where Finn is. Now give me back my hat. If you don't give it back this minute you are all going to stay in after school for the next week.'

The children knew the game was up.

'I don't know where it is, Sir,' said Trixie, holding her hands out in front of her.

She then stepped sideways revealing the bench where Delphi and Scorcher had been sitting.

'There it is,' gasped Mr Turpentine.

He grabbed it with both hands and pulled it over his naked head. The ponytail hung over one ear but Mr Turpentine's drew himself up to his full height and roared,

'Whose lunchbox is this?'

'Mine,' answered Delphi.

'And what is my hat doing there?'

'I don't know.'

'Sir!' said Mr Turpentine.

'Sir,' repeated Delphi.

'She didn't take it, I was with her,' said Scorcher.

'Well, if she didn't take it, who did? Delphi, who took my hair … I mean hat?'

Delphi looked across at Trixie who stared blankly back at her.

'I don't know…Sir.'

'Well, if you don't have the courage to own up, you'd better come with me.'

Delphi's face was pink from anger.

'You will write, '*I must not lie to my teacher*', 500, no, make that 1000 times.'

'1000 lines!' said Turk in disbelief.

'That's a bit over the top,' added Cal.

'Poor Delphi,' said Bela.

'She deserves it,' said Trixie.

'You witch,' spat out Scorcher furiously. 'How could you let Delphi take the blame?'

'She's been a pain ever since she arrived. Messing things up, ruining our friendships.'

'What do you know of friendships. You've never kept a friend for more than five minutes,' snapped Scorcher.

Trixie stuck her tongue out at him and strode away. No-one saw the tears welling in her eyes.

'Why didn't any of you do anything?' continued Scorcher, turning to Turk and Cal.

'She's your girlfriend, Mr Perfect, why didn't you do something?'

'Stop it everyone,' interrupted Bela. 'Don't let's fight. It's over.'

'It's not over, Fuzzy head,' exploded Meg.

'Shut up, Egg head. If you're so clever, you sort it out,' said Turk, and he walked off too.

Cal followed him, kicking the tarmac with his new trainers.

'I loathe you all,' shouted Scorcher.

* * *

The Dream Dealer was spying over the top of the wall. He watched the children blaming each other instead of themselves.

'Deflated balloons. Perfect prey.'

Detentions

I n the detention room, Finn was writing out *'I must not leave the playground in my lunch break'* for the 95th time. He looked up as Mr Turpentine flounced into the room with Delphi. Delphi's eyes widened when she saw Finn but she quickly turned away.

'Sit down. Here's a pen and some paper. Now write, *'I must not lie to my teacher'* 1000 times. Is that clear?' Delphi nodded. 'Keep writing till the bell goes and then come back after school and finish it.'

Mr Turpentine strode out with his wig still askew.

Delphi and Finn immediately looked at each other and grinned.

'What are you doing here?' asked Delphi.

'I went out of the playground.'

'Why?'

'To post a letter.'

'Must have been important. What was it?'

For a moment Finn was silent. Then he said,

'It's just a competition.'

'What do you win?'

Finn shrugged.

'Well, good luck,' said Delphi.

Even when Delphi was being serious, her face looked as if laughter was always just below the surface. Finn liked that. Whenever he had seen himself in the mirror his expression seemed so solemn. He didn't realise that his eyes, like Delphi's, also twinkled humorously.

'So what did you do? Put paint in his coffee?'

'I'll do that tomorrow,' chuckled Delphi.

She quickly explained how Trixie had set her up.

'Why don't you write, '*Trixie took your wig*', 1000 times? Then even Turps might get the point.'

'Everyone would just hate me.'

'I'd have told him. They don't like me anyway,' Finn said without self-pity.

'I don't understand why. I think you're cool.'

Finn's heart didn't miss a beat but he did feel an overwhelming sense of relief. He let out a big sigh as Delphi chatted on,

'Nobody could describe your clothes as cool and your hair looks like you cut it yourself.'

'I did,' he chuckled. 'Someone once said my hair was mouse-coloured. Stupid really. Mice can be lots of different colours.

'That's 'cos it's no particular colour. Mine's blond, Abi's black, Turps has none, and you're mouse – like Hercules.'

'Thanks!' grinned Finn. Then his face became serious. 'I probably shouldn't bring Hercules to school, should I?'

'Course you should. They're just bullies.'

'Hey, you'd better get on with your lines otherwise you'll be here all night.'

'I'll never get them done.'

'You can do them during English. Miss Smelly talks with her eyes closed – just remember to stop writing when she shuts up.'

'Smelly?' giggled Delphi, scribbling hard.

'She's actually called Pelly. She's quite nice – for a teacher,' explained Finn picking up his pen. 'Funny. I'd never have guessed that getting a detention was going to be the best thing that happened to me today.'

The English Lesson

Finn sat next to the window. It overlooked a small alley next to the school kitchens. He had once seen a rat sniffing round it but there was no life out there today.

He noticed Delphi enter the room. She walked past Scorcher and the other kids and sat down next to him. They glanced at each other. She opened her notepad and started writing. There were still 793 lines of her detention to complete during the English class. Neither Finn nor she guessed that she would still have 790 left at the end of the lesson and this was not because Miss Pelly had decided to teach with her eyes open.

Miss Pelly was near retirement age. She wore beige skirts and sensible shoes, but beneath this dull exterior was a woman with a passion. Creative writing. Teaching grammar bored her to the point of *rigor mortis*, particularly having to teach spelling and punctuation, year after year, to the same age group of children who had already learned their texting version of spelling and punctuation and had no desire to learn any other.

'Take a copy of 'English for Dummies 3',' she said, holding up a book. 'Start reading page 15. Adverbs and Adjectives.'

The children collected the books but there was no chance anyone was going to open them. Soon the murmur of complaints and conversation began to sound like a busy Italian restaurant on a Saturday night. Miss Pelly lifted her coffee mug and clanked the metal teaspoon against it. It took a full couple of minutes to get the children's attention.

'What are you all talking about?' she asked. 'Meg. Can you tell me?'

'Um. Just about the weekend, Miss.'

'And you Turk?'

'Same.'

'Is that what you're *all* talking about?' said the teacher.

'Yeah,' mumbled most of the class.

'All right then. Tell me the most exciting thing you discovered during the weekend.'

The room went silent.

'That my sister had nits?' offered Trixie.

'I've been meaning to tell you what I did last holidays,' said Miss Pelly. 'Do you want to know?'

Everyone groaned. Delphi began writing her lines. Miss Pelly closed her eyes and continued regardless.

'I went to Pompeii.'

'Gggggnnnn,' snored Turk.

'I was researching for a film that is being made, based on a novel of that name.'

'A film! Did you get paid lots?' asked Scorcher.

'No. But I was shown something very interesting. A small collection of wax tablets mixed up with some broken pots.'

'What were the tablets for? Diarrhoea?' questioned Bela.

'There were just a few words and phrases written neatly on them but when I began to translate, they turned out to be very interesting.'

'I didn't know you knew Latin!' said Meg.

'In my day you learnt Latin at school.'

'Whatever!' muttered Meg. 'What did they say?'

Miss Pelly opened her eyes and picked up her black notebook.

'Gggggnnnn,' snored Turk again.

'The words were, '...*liquid gold...earth-creature with yellow eyes...alligator skin... crystal jar...Nature trembled angrily...escaped her control...*'

Miss Pelly wrote the words on the white board and then gazed back at the class ecstatically.

'Sorry,' said Scorcher. 'I really don't get what you're on about.'

'I want you to make up a story using these words.

Imagine something that happened in Pompeii, hundreds of years ago. Maybe when Vesuvius erupted. Whatever you like.'

Finn sighed. He was no good at stories. There was enough that was amazing in the real world, like plants that ate meat and birds that decorated their nests with coloured glass. You didn't need to invent anything.

'Trixie, you can start. And whoever is most imaginative can have one of my special brownies.'

Brownies interested Finn and the kids a lot more than telling stories and there was a silence while they all tried hard to think of something.

'*One day a long time ago in Pompeii an alligator escaped from the zoo...*' said Trixie, turning pink under her fake tan. 'I can't think of anything.'

'Your turn,' said Miss Pelly, looking at Scorcher.

'*Ages and ages ago lots of rich people lived in Pompeii. They were so rich that they even had swimming pools filled with liquid gold though nobody swam in them because...*'

'Rubbish,' said Meg and the other kids mumbled their disapproval.

'Your turn, Turk.'

Turk frowned and stared hard at his desk, shutting out the classroom.

'*A kid... was like chucking stones when suddenly a crack appeared in the earth and like out of it struggled this like really weird scary creature...*' Turk paused.

'What did it look like?' questioned Miss Pelly.

'*Well, it had like two legs, two funny little arms, two small horns on its head, an alligator face and like two, yellow eyes.*' Turk looked up and blinked as if he had awoken in bright daylight.

'Can you go on?'

Turk shook his head.

'Well, a brownie for you,' she said carrying the tin over to Turk. 'That's good. That's a proper beginning.'

Turk grinned as he took a bite from the perfectly gooey brownie. He had never been praised in a lesson before.

'Each week you're going to add a bit more. This class is going to tell the Yewton Myth.'

'What's a myth, Mith?' lisped Trixie.

'Something not true,' answered Finn as he collected Hercules from the back of his neck.

'A story with a hidden meaning,' corrected Miss Pelly. 'And if it's as good as I think it will be, then I may include it in the book I am compiling.'

'I didn't know you were writing a book, Miss,' said Meg her eyes sparkling with admiration. 'What's it about?'

'It's a collection of legends and myths from places where a community or civilisation has died out without a proper explanation, like Angkor Wat in Cambodia or Machu Pichu in Peru. I firmly believe our own civilisation and even this community in Yewton is on its way to extinction.'

'What makes you say that?' asked Bela nervously.

'No interest in education, bad manners, no respect…'

The class groaned in unison.

'Murders, mental illness, addictions, dysfunctional families…'

'Speak for yourself,' snapped Trixie.

'I am. I'm speaking for all of us.'

Miss Pelly opened her eyes and looked intensely at each child in the room. 'Please believe me. This is vitally important.'

Delphi stopped writing and Cal gave up puncturing Finn's pencil case with his compass point.

'Those few words, that I have written on the board, recur in all the myths where a civilisation ends.'

'Will you tell us one,' begged Meg.

'No. I don't want to influence your story. There's the bell. Off you go,' ordered Miss Pelly. 'And have some ideas for next week.'

Finn's stomach rumbled as he looked at the tin. How could he ever think of anything imaginative enough to earn him one of those brownies?

Ice-Dreams

A sudden puff of wind scooped up plastic bags and cardboard cartons and blew them hard against the side of the Van. The Dream Dealer understood.

'Clear up the litter, Flake. Mother Nature seems to be in a mood with me.'

'Wwwh-what d'you mean?' asked Flake.

'She and I have a private little war going, don't we?' smirked the Dream Dealer as he brushed the dust off his trousers.

'Why d'you always say M-mother Nature, B-boss?' asked Flake trying to grab a bit of paper.

It escaped from his hand and plastered itself across the Dream Dealer's face.

'Because that's just what She is,' said the Dream Dealer through clenched teeth.

He scrunched up the paper and flung it at Flake.

'An interfering, nagging, tiresome mother. Ever controlling. Convinced of her superiority just because she gave us life.'

He spat on the ground. 'Mothers!'

'I ccccan't remember what my m-mother looked like,' whispered Flake.

'Get an Ice-Dream and cheer up, Flake. We're not babies. We don't need Mother Nature anymore. We've outgrown Her.'

The Dream Dealer observed the wind softening into a breeze and ruffling Finn's hair as he came through the school gates. The boy's mouse had woken up and was crawling out of his sleeve into his hand. The mouse's eyes, like tiny glass beads, stared myopically but his nose busily sniffed the different scents in the air.

'Wait for me, Finn,' called Delphi, as she ran to catch him up. 'Mum's taking me to the new James Bond. D'you want to come?'

'I thought you were going with Scorcher.'

'I was but he's such an idiot. I don't want to talk to him for at least a week.'

'Sorry. I can't. I've got to help Dad clear the drainpipe. I don't want him falling off the ladder,' said Finn.

'Why d'you never talk about your mum?' asked Delphi.

Finn turned to watch a group of younger kids who were standing by the brightly painted Van eating puffy white blobs of ice-cream.

'They look good,' he said.

'Where is your mum?' she persisted.

He was silent.

'Did she die?'

Finn shrugged.

'I'm sorry,' said Delphi.

'It's not your fault,' said Finn.

Delphi gave Hercules a stroke with one finger.

'I've got to go. See you two tomorrow.'

She ran off, turning once to wave.

The Dream Dealer spun round to face the twins.

'Let me guess your names.'

He glanced at Abi's violin case and then closing his eyes, said, 'A... Ab... ABI.'

'Wow!' exclaimed Abi, 'That's amazing.'

'And you must be Jed,' he said, opening his eyes. Abi and her friends squealed delightedly.

The Dream Dealer caught sight of Finn. He waved.

'I'm in a hurry,' said Finn.

'Nice girl,' said the Dream Dealer, indicating Delphi at the end of the street. 'She likes you, doesn't she?'

Finn hesitated.

'You can trust me, young man. I know you're saving up for a puppy but I think you're missing something bigger in your life.'

'Why do you say that?' asked Finn.

'It's my job – to find and fill the missing parts in

people. It's often family bits…'

'Well, there's nothing wrong with *my* family,' responded Finn, a little too forcefully.

'Your mother…'

'Don't talk about my mother,' snapped Finn.

'Poor lad, so you don't have a real, live mother. I've got the finest Mother-Dream. Just the one for you. It's pricey but I couldn't take your money. It's your first ever dream. I'll give it to you free.'

The Dream Dealer knew his words were echoing in Finn's ears. 'Mother-Dream, Mother-Dream, Mother-Dream.' He knew the boy yearned to know what his mother looked like, longed to hear her voice, craved her touch.

'Mother-Dream,' murmured Finn.

And there before him was a huge purple ice, with the colours changing like waves in front of his eyes. Slowly his hand reached out towards the Ice-Dream.

'Ouch!' he yelped, shocked out of his trance by Hercules who had sunk his needle-like teeth into Finn's thumb. 'What did you do that for?'

'Come on, try this. Everyone has the right to know their own mother,' coaxed the Dream Dealer.

'Leave my mother out of it,' Finn shouted, forcing himself away.

'I can help find your mother. Trust me, I can help you.'

The Dream Dealer watched him disappear and then turned his attention to the next arrival. Like a lion watching deer, he was always on the look-out for the one that could be separated from the herd. Scorcher was hanging around the school gates, not sure what to do with himself.

'Don't feel like going home?' questioned the Dream Dealer.

Scorcher glanced up but didn't answer. The Dream Dealer turned his head towards the sign on the Van and Scorcher's eyes automatically followed.

'Ice-Dreams. What are Ice-Dreams?' he whispered.

'Exactly what they say they are. Chilled, pleasant, pleasurable, edible. In a word, 'escape',' murmured the Dream Dealer. 'Isn't that what you feel like?'

Scorcher nodded.

'We all need to get away. Away from the tedium of school, away from tetchy friends, away from purring, prying mothers. Away. Away,' sang out the Dream Dealer while at the same time clicking his fingers sharply at Flake.

After a few anxious seconds, Flake realised what he was meant to do and pulled a large orange and silver ice out of the freezer.

'Have a Utopia. Only a tenner. The world will be yours,' coaxed the Dream Dealer, taking the Ice-Dream from Flake.

Scorcher pulled the money out of his pocket. He reached for the Ice-Dream and took a small, nervous lick. It tasted sweet as honey and yet had the sharp tang of a tangerine. As he took another lick, the Dream Dealer watched as all the tightness and tension, worries and irritations, anger and anxiety flowed out of Scorcher's body.

Ice-Dreams seemed to put you in a bubble. A large multi-coloured bubble like the ones you make with washing-up liquid. A gentle protective membrane lay between Scorcher and the outside world. He looked at the other children in the distance, and glowed with warmth, as if they were all his best friends. Everything was going to be all right between him and Delphi. The Dream Dealer smiled supportively.

Cal was watching from a distance. Suddenly the ball he was carrying seemed to fly out of his arms. The Dream Dealer caught it neatly on the end of his black boot. He balanced it on his toe as if it was fixed with superglue, then he kicked it from toe to toe a few times and flicked it back to Cal.

Cal was captivated. He edged towards the Van.

'This is the best,' said Scorcher, swaying slightly.

'What is it?' asked Cal.

'You must have heard of Ice-Dreams. They're really cool.'

'Obviously. They're made of ice,' replied Cal defensively.

Scorcher laughed and laughed. Cal looked at him suspiciously. Even he didn't think what he'd said was so funny.

'No seriously, I know all about them,' giggled Scorcher. 'You eat them and then your dream comes true. Isn't that right?' he added turning to the Dream Dealer.

'Spot on, Scorcher. Bright lad.'

Cal's face had set in a half smile. He stood frozen between fear and longing.

'Try one,' said Scorcher. 'Come on. They're great.'

But Cal shook his head and began backing away.

The Dream Dealer recognised the signs. Fear was like a hungry crocodile. He knew what to feed it. He faced Cal and slowly removed his dark glasses. His features blurred into a shapeless ball of reptilian flesh. His eyes blazed and bored deep into the back of the boy's head. Cal gasped, his breath trapped in his chest.

'Have a Survivor,' hissed the Dream Dealer, his tongue flicking viper-like. 'A deliciousssss Sssssssurvivor.'

He held the lurid lime-green ice close to Cal. 'Irressssssistible. Try it. Go on. Try it.'

Without taking his eyes from the hideous creature, Cal obediently licked the Ice-Dream. He closed his eyes and slowly exhaled. It tasted fresh and clean and sweet. He was safe.

'Girls won't seem so scary after one of these,' said the Dream Dealer gently.

He stepped away, his face returned to human-form, his dark glasses once more covering his eyes.

Relief flashed across Cal's face. The Dream Dealer understood him. He was encircled by the peaceful bubble. Everything felt all right. Everything felt possible.

The Dream Dealer let out a contemptuous sigh. Sometimes it was too easy. He watched the little Earth-imp staring at a row of bottles in the Van, her whole body tense with anticipation. As Scorcher and Cal had bought Ice-Dreams, their names had instantly appeared, elegantly engraved, in the glass. And as they ate the ices part of their inner selves had flowed out of them and been stored as coloured vapour.

But the Earth-imp was interested only in finding twins. And not just any twins. They had to be a girl and a boy and they had to be 'perfect', their souls light enough to balance with the feather on the scales. She had stamped her foot with impatience when Abi and Jed had left without buying an Ice-Dream. Without twins she could not enter the human dimension.

'I'll get you your twins, my little one, don't you worry,' whispered the Dream Dealer.

The Answer

Weeks passed and Finn waited impatiently for a reply to his letter. It finally arrived one Saturday morning. It was two lines long and said that unless he could supply more information, such as his mother's name, they were unable to assist him further. He ripped it up. It came through the letterbox with two other brown printed envelops addressed to John Greenstock.

'Why do we always get bills to John Greenstock?' asked Finn.

'Must have lived here before us,' answered his dad. 'Give them to me. I'll deal with them.'

'Do I have any grandparents?'

'No. They died years ago.'

'Where was I born?'

'What difference does it make?'

'Where was I born?'

'London. Now stop these questions, Finn. You know it drives me mad.'

'Well, having no answers drives me mad,' thought Finn but he knew better than to say it. At least he had found out one thing. His mum certainly had to have been in London when he was born.

* * *

'Have you ever been to London?' Finn asked Delphi, as they were leaving school next day.

'Yer, when we first came over. We went on the London Eye. It goes really slowly.'

'What's London like?'

'Huge. I'd never find my way around. It took hours and hours getting out of it. Why d'you ask?' said Delphi, noticing Finn's frown. 'What are you thinking?'

'Nothing,' he said, while his head throbbed with frustration.

How could he ever have thought that he could find his mother in London?

'You're so secretive,' said Delphi. 'It's really irritating. Sometimes I feel I've known you forever and sometimes I don't think I know you at all.'

'Well you're like being with a...with a policeman. Questions. Questions. Questions. Why d'you have to be so nosey?' retorted Finn.

He hated being called secretive. Hated it because

it was true. His tummy felt all tight. Delphi had blown into his life like a spring breeze and here he was polluting everything – a truck spewing out diesel fumes. He was sick at himself.

'I know I'm curious. Sorry,' said Delphi, glancing at Finn's screwed up face.

'I'm sorry I'm secretive,' he muttered.

They walked towards the chestnut tree. Starry white blossoms burst from every branch. A bumble bee bounced onto one of the candle-like flowers, bending it alarmingly to one side. Finn reached up and picked a leaf. With his thumb and middle finger, he skilfully stripped out the green bits.

'That's amazing,' she said. 'It's like the skeleton of a fish.'

Finn picked another leaf and handed it to her. She concentrated hard, trying to copy what she had seen him do, but some of the ribs tore. She chucked it on the ground.

They walked on in silence. Neither heard the cars nor noticed the people that walked past with their kids and shopping bags. Hercules woke and ran up Finn's sleeve, tickling his neck. He had forgotten all about him. He automatically picked the mouse out of his shirt and deposited him up his sleeve again. A low wall ran along the row of houses. Without saying a word they both sat on it.

'How d'you know I was going to do that?' laughed Delphi.

'I didn't. I didn't even know I was going to sit down – till I sat down,' said Finn.

'I've been meaning to ask you – what happened about that competition you entered. I s'pose you didn't win anything?' asked Delphi.

'No, I didn't.'

Finn swung one of his legs, kicking his heel against the wall over and over. How could he be lying again? And to Delphi whom he liked more than anyone else, except his dad. What was wrong with him? Some people bit their nails and couldn't stop. He lied.

'If you want to know...I didn't enter a competition.'

Delphi was confused but she forced herself to keep quiet.

'It wasn't true what I just said. I didn't know you very well then and I didn't know whether I could trust you.' He continued to kick the wall. 'It wasn't a competition, it was a letter to a place in London who I thought could tell me something about my mother. They couldn't.'

'Is that why you were asking about London, just now?'

'Sort of. The only thing I know for definite is that I must have been with her when I was born. And I was born in London. But it doesn't help...she could be in...in Africa by now or be ...'

'I'm sure she's not dead,' interrupted Delphi.

'You can't be sure. You just hope she's alive. So do I. But maybe that's just wishful thinking.'

Delphi let out a big sigh.

'And another thing I lied about was Dad.'

'Are you going to tell me he really *is* a burglar?' Delphi said, almost making Finn smile.

'D'you remember I said his job didn't pay much. Well, he doesn't have a job. He's on the dole. Things are pretty tight at home.'

A large blob of white landed on Delphi's knee. They both stared at it and then their eyes looked up at the sky.

'Was that a pigeon?' said Delphi, with her face screwed up in disgust. 'I can't believe what it just did. And there it is flying off as if nothing's happened.'

'It's meant to be lucky,' said Finn, trying to keep his face serious.

He picked up a bit of paper from the street and tried to wipe it off.

'Lucky! Are you joking. It's revolting!'

They both started laughing.

'If that happened when I was with Scorcher, I'd die of embarrassment.'

'Why?' Finn asked.

'Dunno. I s'pose it's 'cos I'm trying to impress him. Silly isn't it? Whereas with you, it's just really funny.'

'Is that meant to be a compliment?'

'It's true,' said Delphi, standing up. 'Look, you've

smudged it all over me. I'm going home to wash.'

'Let's hope it brings you some luck.'

'It'd better. Maybe I'll find your mum,' said Delphi. 'See you tomorrow.'

And she was gone.

Finn jumped high in the air. Then remembering Hercules, he took the mouse in his hand and kissed him.

'I feel as light as you, Hercules. Let's go.'

They raced off to Alf's house.

Guarding the Gates

T' here weren't only things at home that Finn didn't understand. Something strange was also going on at school. It had started with Scorcher and Cal and then, like a virus, had spread to some of the other kids. There was a lot of whispering and furtive trips to the Ice-cream Van.

Scorcher paid Finn to stand guard at the school gates and whistle if he saw a grown-up. The more Finn observed the Dream Dealer, the more intrigued he became. How did this man entice the kids to confess their innermost thoughts? Finn kept overhearing his classmates telling him things about themselves that he would never have believed.

Trixie had chucked a bit of screwed-up paper and called him a 'waste bin' as she walked out of the gates. Then minutes later he had heard her saying to the Dream Dealer,

'Why do I only feel good when I put someone down? I hate it.'

The Dream Dealer had quickly reassured her that a Mystic Bean would stop her feeling threatened and allow her to be as nice as she really was. And Finn had to admit that she was more bearable when she had eaten a Mystic Bean.

Another day he had seen Turk sidling up to the Dream Dealer and saying he didn't want everyone to know his dream.

'Quite right,' the Dream Dealer had said. 'There's more power in secrets. I'm here to help. Trust me'

'I'm thick. I hate always being bottom,' Turk had admitted.

'I understand. I've helped plenty like you,' the Dream Dealer had answered confidentially. 'Flake! Have we got a Starry Surrender?'

Turk had eaten it but Finn didn't notice him moving up in class. In fact, once he got into Ice-Dreams, Turk often missed class altogether.

Sometimes the Dream Dealer would glance towards Finn as if he wanted him to hear what was being said. But Finn always pretended not to be listening.

'Could I get straight hair,' Bela asked quietly.

'Fat chance,' thought Finn.

'Easy. I've got just the one for you, young lady. Only £3.50.'

'Rubbish,' said a girl from Bela's group of

admirers. 'Come on. I'm getting out of here.'

'It's a free world,' said the Dream Dealer, handing Bela an Ice-Dream. 'What beautiful earrings. You're a lady with taste.'

Bela visibly expanded with the Dream Dealer's attention.

At that minute Finn noticed a mother with two kids leaving the school and approaching the Van. He whistled and Flake quickly switched the sign from Ice-Dreams to Ice-creams. The mother bought three ice-creams from Flake. Finn watched her ruffle one of the kid's hair and then take their hands as they walked away. His heart contracted.

*　　*　　*

Finn never mentioned the Dream Dealer to Delphi. He was afraid if he told her what he had seen and heard, she wouldn't believe him.

'We're going skate-boarding this afternoon. Come with us,' begged Delphi one day when lessons ended. 'You can borrow my board.'

'Thanks but I can't,' answered Finn, wishing he could.

'Didn't see your mum and dad at the parents' meeting last night,' shouted Bela to Finn, making sure everyone could hear. Finn put his head down and squeezed his ears shut.

'Finn doesn't have parents, do you Finn? You live

in an orphanage, isn't that right?' giggled Meg.

'He has a mouse instead of a family,' said Turk.

'Go on Finn tell us where you mum and dad are, or don't you have any?' persisted Cal, standing in front of Finn.

'Mum works at night and sleeps all day, and Dad travels all the time. Now get out of my way,' said Finn.

Delphi winked at him. With her on his side, he didn't care what the kids said.

'They obviously don't get paid, that's for sure,' said Scorcher.

'Why do you say that?' said Delphi, glaring at him. However much she fancied Scorcher, she wasn't going to stay silent if he bullied Finn.

'Only joking. I mean, he doesn't exactly have the latest gear, does he?'

Finn had moved on and Delphi ran to catch up with him.

'Please come with us.'

'I'm taking Alf's dogs for a walk. Thanks anyway.'

'I'm going back in to find Mum. She's been stuffing letters and sticking stamps all day.'

'At school? Does she get paid?' asked Finn, thinking he could offer to do the same.

'No.'

'Why does she do it then?'

'Never asked. She always does it. Whatever school I'm at,' answered Delphi. 'See you.'

As Finn started out of the Playground, he found

Scorcher beside him.

'Guard the gates, Finn. Whistle if you see an oldie,' he whispered.

'Guard them yourself. You haven't paid me for a week,' answered Finn.

'Oh man, don't be so mean. I've spent all my money...'

'On Ice-Dreams.'

'So? I'll pay you next week. Promise.'

But Finn couldn't be persuaded and he walked away leaving Scorcher showering his back with insults.

As Finn passed the Van he heard the Dream Dealer's familiar voice.

'Still no luck finding your mother? You mustn't give up. You're not going to have any peace till you find out what happened to her.'

Finn tried to shut out the words but it was impossible because they were echoing the thoughts in his head.

'I lost my brother for years and years and I found him. In fact I've helped dozens of people find loved ones. It's a bit of a speciality of mine.'

Finn continued walking but the last words he heard were,

'You can't always do things by yourself. I have a network of friends who can help. Let me know when you're ready...'

The Experiment

'Time for the Experiment,' said the Dream Dealer checking his watch. 'You've got the Old Bag lined up for 4 o'clock, have you, Flake?'

'Pppp-promised her steak and chips like you said, B-boss.'

'Don't look glum. It saves me so much time. Nothing like giving people a choice. Then you can see what they're made off.'

The Dream Dealer carefully poured sunflower oil onto the pavement. As he looked up, the first of his target group began wandering out of the school gates and making their way to the Van.

'She's ccccoming now, B-boss,' whispered Flake as the Dream Dealer handed him the empty plastic bottle.

Down the street, a shapeless bundle was

hobbling towards them. The Old Bag, as the Dream Dealer called her, was draped in layers of discarded clothing. On her head sat a battered straw sunhat, beneath which a wrinkled face muttered and swore to itself. Her feet were sockless and squashed into ill-fitting shoes and her arms were stretched by the weight of countless plastic bags containing her worldly possessions. Limping and staggering behind her came the little Earth-imp. She knew her grotesque imitation of the Old Bag would entertain the Dream Dealer.

'Anyone want a Utopia?' asked Scorcher.

'Will you share a Fancy Fish, Cal,' said Turk. 'I've only got a quid.'

'Don't let's hang around here,' moaned Meg. 'Let's go to the park like we said.'

The Dream Dealer joined his little Earth-imp. As the Old Bag neared the patch of oil, he gave her a forceful shove. She stumbled into the oil. Her two feet skidded from under her, plastic bags flew in the air, her arms waved like windmills and then – crash – she was on the ground. Her layers of clothes had softened the blow of landing but they also made it impossible for her to get up. She lay like a cockroach cast on its back, legs thrashing helplessly in the air.

'Disgusting, smelly Old Bag,' muttered the Dream Dealer. 'If I had bigger feet, I'd crush her like an insect. Put her out of her misery. Leave the world a better place.'

He left the little Earth-imp curled up in a heap of spiteful laughter while he positioned himself to monitor the next phase of his Experiment. He watched and waited. Out of the corner of one of his ever-alert eyes, he noticed a teacher coming out of the school gates, followed by a straggling group of younger children.

'All I need,' he cursed. 'This never happens at 4 o'clock on a Tuesday.'

But he need not have worried. The teacher was Mr Turpentine. He was gesturing wildly and bellowing,

'Hurry along, everyone. Keep up. Keep up.'

As Turps neared the Old Bag, he turned to the kids in his Art Club and shouted,

'Use your eyes. Be alert. Observe every detail. Look at that tree. Look! What colour do you think the leaves are?'

Some of the kids watched Mr Turpentine, fascinated by his gesticulations. Others stared at the writhing, groaning heap of clothes on the pavement. Only one child looked at the tree and answered,

'Green, of course.'

'Of course NOT,' cried Mr T. triumphantly. 'You think leaves are green because that's what you're taught. Look at the ones in the shadow – they're not green, they are…browney, purpley black and observe …' His voice faded away as he continued down the street. The Dream Dealer smiled scornfully. He could trust Mr Turpentine not to notice anything.

Meg kept glancing at the Bag Lady and then back at her friends. She was torn. The Dream Dealer could read her expression like a magazine. He'd seen it many times before. She wanted to help but she was afraid. The Bag Lady was dirty and heavy and maybe a bit crazy. It would be embarrassing. Her friends would tease her. Finally, Meg could no longer bear the sight of the old woman struggling. She took one last look at her friends and ran away.

'Mmm! Interesting,' murmured the Dream Dealer to the Earth-imp. 'She could be for us.'

The Dream Dealer slunk further into the shadow as he saw his next subject enter his Experiment. It was Finn. The boy was engrossed in watching Hercules attacking a mint, the mouse's teeth working like a tiny pneumatic drill.

Within seconds Finn was aware of an unfamiliar sound – someone was in distress. Without hesitating, Finn hurried towards the Bag Lady, pushing Hercules and the mint into his pocket. He struggled through the wads of material and managed to loop his arms under the old lady's armpits. He levered her inelegantly into a sitting position. She sat muttering and swearing at him. It reminded him of when he had saved a pigeon from being run over for a second time. The pigeon had pecked him so hard it had drawn blood.

'There's oil here – that's why you slipped. Are you hurt?' he asked.

She didn't answer. She grabbed hold of his arm and nearly pulled him over as she struggled to stand up. He held his breath as a waft of her stinking clothes reached his nose.

'Is that your granny?' asked Trixie.

'Might be for all I know,' thought Finn.

'Ooooh! Look at God's little helper,' Turk mocked.

'What would you like me to do?' retorted Finn. 'Chop her up with a chain-saw. That make you happy?'

Turk blinked and turned away. He took a large bite out of his Fancy Fish.

'You okay?' Finn asked, picking up the plastic bags and handing them to the old lady.

She didn't answer. She took a large alarm clock out of one of the bags and flung it at the Van. It missed and lay on the ground with the alarm ringing.

'Give her an ice-cream, Flake,' called the Dream Dealer. 'She's had a nasty shock.'

But the Old Bag didn't want anything more to do with Flake or the Dream Dealer. She hobbled back the way she had come, her distrust in mankind confirmed.

The Dream Dealer had enjoyed every minute. The Experiment had gone perfectly. He would write, 'Result as predicted. Finn for my Jar.'

Eavesdropping

It was not only Finn who refused to buy an Ice-Dream, the twins were also proving hard to win over. When the Dream Dealer had managed to convince Abi he could make her into a famous violinist, Jed had persuaded her not to buy a dream. And when Jed had been tempted to become a rock star, then Abi had called him a hypocrite and had threatened to tell their parents.

One Sunday afternoon, as the Dream Dealer reached for the Jar to help him retain his human appearance, he noticed Jed and Abi playing in a street not far from the Van.

'You've got a problem with those twins,' commented Flake.

'I don't have problems,' growled the Dream Dealer watching the wrinkles beginning to appear on his hands.

'Why do some kids not want the ices, B-boss?' continued Flake bravely.

'A hundred different reasons. They all want them in the end and that's what counts.'

'I s'pose some are scared of trying nnnew things.'

'Hmm. Scared,' mused the Dream Dealer, noticing a ladder leaning against a building. Jed was rushing towards it, shouting a challenge to his twin.

'Watch me go under it!'

'Don't you dare,' begged Abi. She turned and walked away to discourage him.

'I broke that mirror and nothing happened. It's all rubbish. Watch!'

Jed marched defiantly under the rungs of the ladder. Something leapt out in front of him. He jumped. The Dream Dealer, unrecognisably hideous, paralysed him with the force of his eyes. Jed's feet wouldn't move. He opened his mouth to scream but no sound came out. The Dream Dealer's features had transformed into a scaley-skinned maggot. His lips were curled back to reveal yellow fangs and the air smelt foul as he opened his mouth and hissed,

'Assassin! Hassss no-one told you the ssstupidity of defying sssssupersssstition? Ssshe'll die. Your precious ssssister will DIE!'

The last word boomed inside Jed's head as if it were ricocheting round a mountain range. Die! Die! Die! Die! He closed his eyes trying to blot out the noise and the gruesome apparition. Gradually the familiar sound of traffic and voices returned. He opened his eyes. There was nothing there. His whole body was trembling. He put his hand against the building and retched.

'Poor child. What on earth's happened to you? You look like you've seen a ghost,' said a comforting voice.

'I did,' mumbled Jed. He gazed up into the concerned, human face of the Dream Dealer.

'Did you walk under that ladder?' he asked, casually cleaning the lenses of his dark glasses on a black silk handkerchief.

Jed nodded, sick with terror at what he had done.

'Not good. Not good at all. You'd better come with me,' he said, putting on his glasses and leading the boy to the Van.

'You must have a Viper's Venom to undo the curse. Quick, Flake, quick. No time to waste.' The Dream Dealer grabbed an acid-green ice and handed it to Jed. Without hesitation, he began to lick. He was thinking only of his twin.

'Jed. WHAT are you doing?' asked Abi, returning to the Van. 'Are you crazy?'

But the Ice-Dream had already begun to have its effect. Jed was in his own pleasant bubble. He had forgotten the terrifying vision. He had forgotten the death-threat. He had even forgotten the ladder until Abi reminded him.

'I told you if you walked under that ladder something bad would happen,' said Abi looking at her twin with disbelief.

'And it didn't.'

'It did. Look at you. You've got one of those dreadful Ice-Dreams. You've gone all weird like the others.'

'Everything's fantastic,' mused Jed.

'It's not. You're crazy.'

'Okay. Okay. It's not and I'm crazy,' agreed Jed.

'Come on. We'd better go home,' said Abi miserably.

'You see, Flake. No problem,' said the Dream Dealer.

*   *   *

The little Earth-imp sat guarding the bottle marked Jed with its pink and blue striped vapour. At last a twin. She nervously bit her claws. Was she nearing the time when she could join the human dimension? And was the Dream Dealer's dream, also, about to be realised? The Jar had almost reached the infinity symbol. Any time now the vapour would transmute into the breath of eternal life. And then what? Would he forget her? Nature was sending up increasing numbers of earth-imps. Every week seemed to bring another tsunami or tornado. What if he found some other earth-imp and decided to humanise her?

'Now for Abi,' said the Dream Dealer, pouring himself a glass of iced white wine and settling himself in a comfortable deck chair in the afternoon sun. The Earth-imp climbed onto the Dream Dealer's shoulder and gazed beseechingly into his eyes. Her greatest pleasure was to hear the stories of how he evolved from being an ordinary earth-imp like her. His greatest pleasure was talking about himself.

'All right, little one, I'm in the mood,' he said, removing his gloves and stroking her.

'*Old Vesuvius was rumbling, grumbling and on the verge of erupting when our dear Mother Nature, once again, chose me to be the bearer of the Jar of Gold.*'

He chuckled maliciously and the Little Earth-imp grinned back.

'*I clawed my way to the surface, where the earth touches space, and gazed around. All at once my whole being was overcome by a spasm of envy. Why should Nature control me and keep me from such a wondrous world? But I was Her slave, so I automatically headed for the City of Pompeii.*

'*I'd always found human life attractive, I'd even been quite happy to help them.*

'*But on that particular day I understood why. Humans are free, unlike earth-imps or the rest of earth's creatures. They can choose whether to use Mother Nature and all She has to offer. But they are equally free to abuse Her. Humans bend Her laws. They enjoy Her beauty when it suits them. They plunder Her riches from beneath the earth and ravage those above. And what can She do? Nothing. That's why I admired and envied them.*'

The Dream Dealer took a mouthful of wine and then poured a drop into the little Earth-imp's cupped claws. She lapped it up and waited for the Dream Dealer to continue.

'As the volcano erupted and the suffocating cloud of ash started to fall on the city, a brilliant idea came into my mind. Instead of leading the terrified people to safety, I decided to do something different. I hid the precious Jar and left the screaming, shrieking mob to their fate.

'Why not use the liquid gold for myself?'

The Earth-imp's eyes glistened with excitement. She was so enraptured by the story that she failed to notice they were not alone.

* * *

Finn hadn't felt like going home and watching TV. He wanted to visit the Van. Would the Dream Dealer mention his mother again?

At first, Finn presumed the Dream Dealer was talking to someone on his mobile. Then he realised the man was alone. Finn hid behind the Van and listened.

'I travelled to Rome and on the way I made a collection of mouth-watering jewels from the gold. I believed that if I could make loads of money then I could have anything I wished for.'

Finn hardly dared breathe.

'I laid my wares on the ground near a water fountain

and waited. But when the first greedy people arrived, they looked around and then began to help themselves. That was when I realised I was invisible to them. I bit and I scratched crazily to defend my jewels. I can only presume they thought it was their conscience pricking them, because it wasn't long before they were putting money in the Jar in exchange for the jewels.'

'Jar!' thought Finn.

'Then something much more important happened which, at the time, I did not fully understand. A young girl, very pretty and expensively dressed, fell in love with my jewels. Happy to deceive her nursemaid, she asked her to fetch her a drink from the fountain. As soon as the woman's back was turned, the girl stole a pair of delicate heart-shaped earrings and hid them in her pocket. As I was about to attack her, I noticed a small pink cloud floating in the Jar. I didn't know what it meant but I sensed it was important. I knew I must keep the Jar beside me.'

'What's he talking about? Who's he talking to? What's going on?' thought Finn.

'My first mistake had been to believe that money could buy anything. I soon discovered it couldn't. Money could not give me the thing I desired most – to be a human. For that I needed something indefinable, unseeable, untouchable. I needed the very essence of a human. I needed their soul. That was when I remembered the pink cloud that had appeared in the crystal Jar and in a flash I understood.

'When a child takes something from me they lose a little bit of themselves.'

Finn gasped.

'That precious essence somehow held the power to transform me. But I was still invisible ...'

The little Earth-imp had leapt off the Dream Dealer's shoulder and hurried to look round the side of the Van. The Dream Dealer quickly followed her.

Finn was struggling to make sense of what he was hearing, when, suddenly, looming in front of him appeared the Dream Dealer's face.

'What are you doing here?'

Finn jumped, sending Hercules flying out of his sleeve.

'Nothing.'

Finn bent down and grabbed Hercules as he scuttled away from the Dream Dealer.

'Eavesdropping, were you?'

'Why were you talking to yourself?' retorted Finn.

The Dream Dealer hesitated briefly.

'Who else have I got to talk to? Flake isn't exactly the brightest.'

'Is it a myth?' said Finn, realising there had to be some connection with Miss Pelly's story.

'That's exactly what it is. A myth. A famous myth,' replied the Dream Dealer. 'Heard it on my travels.'

Finn didn't want to prolong the conversation. Something about the Dream Dealer always made him want to run. He needed to get home and remind himself of the story he had just heard. Maybe it would help him earn a brownie.

'And I haven't forgotten about your mum,' shouted the Dream Dealer as Finn raced away down the street.

*　　*　　*

'I need that kid,' he muttered.

The little Earth-imp looked at him questioningly.

'His soul will certainly balance on the scales but something tells me his vapour may even be gold. That would hurry things up.'

The little Earth-imp scowled and scratched her nails against the bottle marked Jed.

Finn didn't interest her.

Alf's Dogs

Aside from his friendship with Delphi, Finn's happiest moments were spent at Alf's house. It looked like all the others in the row but out the back, through the kitchen door, lay a tiny patch of countryside. Alf called it his paradise. When it rained the soil smelled of earth not dust, when he mowed the square of lawn the cuttings gave off the summery scent of real grass and, when he let Finn eat one of his carefully nurtured tomatoes, it was warm and tasted of sweetness and sunshine.

The most precious thing in Alf's garden was his ash tree. It had seeded itself eleven years ago, shortly after his wife had died. He told Finn that over time it would grow too big. Its roots would spread in all directions, destroying the wall, the house and probably breaking up the pavement and road beyond, but it wouldn't happen till long after he was gone. For now Alf was content to water and tend it, and each winter he firmly cut back its branches to keep it from bothering the neighbours.

Finn's favourite times were when one of Alf's Shetland sheepdogs would have puppies. They were pedigree dogs and people would pay hundreds of pounds for each one. Finn had often noticed how owners resembled their dogs but he didn't think Alf looked at all like a Sheltie, he looked more like a pug with his short legs and snub nose that wrinkled up when he laughed, which he did a lot. Twice a week, after school, Finn would take Alf's dogs for a walk in the park.

He and Alf were good friends. They would chat together about the dogs and the money Finn was saving and the jobs that needed doing like watering the plants or mixing the food or brushing the dogs.

'Alf?' asked Finn. 'Have you ever bought a dream?'

'That's an odd question, me duk.'

Alf always called Finn, 'My duck' because that's what his gran had called him when he was a boy.

'Pass me them dog leads, would you.'

'The thing about dreams is they don't last,' continued Finn, taking the leads off the hook behind the door.

'Nice while you're 'aving 'em though,' smiled Alf.

'Yea – but even when they're nice, you still have to wake up and get on with reality.'

'I had a funny 'un last week. Dreamt I found a

lump o' gold in a pile o' muck. I gave it a wash and there it was, pure as anything.'

Alf struggled to remember what happened next. But, as he said, the harder you try to remember a dream, the farther away it slips.

'Anyway, I don't think it sounds too good *buying* dreams,' Alf chuckled. 'The whole point of 'em is they have to be yer own.'

'That's exactly what I said … I mean, think,' agreed Finn, remembering his conversation with the Dream Dealer.

'Hey, me duk, meant to tell yer, the vet thinks Alice is carrying quite a few pups this time,' commented Alf as he put a lead on the plumpest of the two dogs. 'So maybe she'll 'ave a runt.'

Finn felt a flutter of excitement and he knelt down and gently stroked Alice. Without looking up he asked,

'If you'd lost someone, Alf, how would you go about looking for them?'

'You're full a questions today, me duk,' said Alf scratching his head. 'I've lost me glasses often enough but I don't think I've ever lost any*body*. Why d'you ask? 'Ave you lost someone?'

'No. But I know someone who has.'

'When I lost one of me dogs I went to the police and put an ad in the local paper. Suppose they could try that.'

'It's no good,' thought Finn.

Alf handed Finn the dogs on their leads and told him he had crumpets and honey for tea. The dogs were barking and jumping about but Finn, using a firm voice, soon had them under control. They looked at him expectantly. Finn was thinking about something else and his feet set off automatically in the direction of the Ice-cream Van.

*　　*　　*

Meg had hung around the Van for the last week. She had watched her friends buying dreams and laughing at things she didn't find funny. It was all very well being clever but she also wanted to be cool and part of the gang.

'Join in or go away,' they said to her. But she didn't do either. She was afraid of things she didn't understand and nobody could explain what made an Ice-Dream.

'Ah, the bright one,' said a reassuring voice. The Dream Dealer came towards her and stopped. She wanted to leave but her feet wouldn't move.

'The one who asks the questions. The one who wants to bury her past and make tomorrow her own.'

'How do you know?' she said. 'Who are you? What are these dreams. I don't understand what they do to you? I don't...' Meg could have asked another ten questions but the Dream Dealer interrupted her.

'Sometimes the more you think the less you understand. Trust me. I've got what you need.'

Meg didn't trust him but she was fed up with being different.

'Flake! One Beauty Queen for this young lady.'

Flake lumbered over with a pink and silver Ice-Dream and Meg reached out for it, relieved that a decision had been made. She took a lick and tasted the cold, sweet berry flavour. The soft bubble enclosed her and through it she saw the kind smiling face of the Dream Dealer and her friends calling her over. She felt like a drop of rain when it joins other drops and forms a pool. She was no longer separate and alone but part of something bigger.

* * *

The little Earth-imp began leaping frantically up and down on the roof of the Van.

'FLAKE!' yelled the Dream Dealer. 'THE SIGN!'

Delphi who was sitting by the entrance to the playground waiting for her mother watched with interest as Flake hurried to the Van and with a quick flick changed the D to C, so that Ice-Dream read as Ice-Cream. At that minute a car drew up with Jed and Abi in the back seat and their parents in the front. Delphi could hear them arguing through the open window. The father was saying,

'I've had enough of all this nonsense, Abi. There

is no such thing as 'Ice-Dreams'. I don't know why I bother to send you to school if they don't even teach you how to read.' He got angrily out of the car and went up to Flake.

'Four vanilla ices, please.'

Flake whistled merrily as he made them, while the Dream Dealer faded into the shadows.

'Ice-CREAMS, all right everybody,' said the father, pointing to the sign. He handed the ices through the window and climbed into the car. Abi started crying.

Delphi was intrigued. What were these Ice-Dreams? And why was it a secret from the grown-ups? She went over to Meg and Bela who were laughing together.

'What's the joke?' asked Dephi.

'What's flat and red and goes up and down in a lift?' said Meg.

'A squashed tomato,' giggled Bela.

Delphi groaned.

'Try an Ice-Dream. I promise you, everything's so funny.'

'I'd better not. My mum will be here in a minute and she'd kill me.'

'Why? What's wrong with dreams?' asked Bela.

'I don't know. It's just that man doesn't seem to want the grown-ups to know.'

'Of course he doesn't. Grown-ups ruin everything. They don't see things as they are, they see them as they think they're meant to be,' said Meg.

Delphi thought of how Abi and Jed's father had disbelieved them. An ice-cream van could be only an ice-cream van, as far as he was concerned. Dreams did not exist. Meg was right. Grown-ups could be very stupid. Perhaps she should give it a go. Delphi started looking at the different names on the Van: Magical Sun, Mystic Bean, Utopia...'

'Try a Zany Zest. Good clean fun,' tempted the Dream Dealer, emerging out of the shadows. 'You'll laugh till your sides ache.'

Delphi reached into her pocket to get change, smiling with excitement. As she did so she noticed Finn coming down the road, the dogs dragging his arms straight. Suddenly the dogs stopped and sniffed, their hackles rising. Then they turned and bolted, their leads catapulting Finn's legs into the air. The leads flew out of his hands and the dogs were gone.

A gust of wind stung the Dream Dealer's face. He knew whose work this was. Even in the centre of town, Nature was uncomfortably close.

Delphi pulled Finn to his feet and they dashed after the dogs.

'Alice, Digby, come back. Alice! Digby! Here!' A car just missed them. They raced down a side street.

'Alice! Wait!'

The dogs stopped. They turned towards Finn and their tails, which had been pinned between their legs, reappeared and started wagging again.

'Good dogs,' said Finn, picking up their leads and patting them.

'I thought they were going to get run over,' panted Delphi, as she caught up with him. 'What on earth gave them such a fright?'

'It must have been that Dream Dealer,' said Finn. 'Normally they bark at strangers. I've never, ever seen them run away like that.'

'That was really odd,' agreed Delphi. 'Ask Alf what he thinks.'

'I know what he'll say. He'll say that if the dogs are scared of someone, you should be too.'

'Really! I'd like to meet Alf. Have you told him about us being friends?'

'No,' said Finn.

He paused.

'Sometimes when something is really special you don't want to share it. You don't want anyone to spoil it.'

'I know. That's exactly why I've hardly told Mum anything about you. She'd ask so many questions.'

'Sounds like you.'

'Don't say that,' laughed Delphi. 'If I ever have kids, will you remind me not to keep questioning them?'

'With pleasure.'

'I'd better run in case mum's waiting. Bye Digby. Bye Alice.'

*   *   *

Finn watched Delphi shrinking into the distance. He tried to imagine what it would be like to have your mum waiting for you.

The Lucky Break

Finn had tasted his first ever brownie and he was determined it would not be his last. The Yewton Myth was growing week by week and Finn's contribution of the crystal Jar containing the essence of a child earned high praise from Miss Pelly. She said it had 'real mythic quality' and that maybe he would be a writer one day. Finn couldn't imagine anything worse than being a writer but he managed to keep his face serious.

Delphi had been impressed. He told her it hadn't come from his own imagination but when she tried to find out where he had got his ideas from, he refused to say.

'I don't want to tell you,' he said. 'Don't ask, okay?'

So she didn't.

Scorcher had described in technicoloured detail how he had seen the street flowing past him like a river with the sound of water rushing and tumbling so loudly that he had had to block his ears. The buildings around him had grown and grown until he, and all the people around, had shrunk to the size of ants. His description had won him two brownies.

Miss Pelly was determined to encourage their efforts and promised she would take the most imaginative pupils to a meal at Pizza Palace. Finn was the only one in the class who had never been there. He knew where he would have to go to get some more ideas.

'Mighty Scream. Fancy Fish. Only a fiver. Cheap at the price,' called out Flake, as Finn approached the Van. Finn waved and walked past to where the Dream Dealer stood eyeing the world through his shades.

'Can I help?' he enquired, drawing on his cigar.

'I want to hear some more of your myths,' said Finn. 'They're good.'

'Enjoy fantasy do you?'

'Not usually.'

'Just my kind of fantasy, eh? I like that,' said the Dream Dealer, pleased to have lured Finn back. 'So what shall we have today? Shall we tell the one about the Earth-imp's lucky break?'

The little Earth-imp was climbing up his boot. This was her favourite story. If it had been possible she would have purred.

'Make yourself comfortable,' said the Dream Dealer, settling himself in his deck chair and poking the end of his cigar with a match.

'Once upon a time an earth-imp was journeying through the scrub and bushlands of deepest Africa. He had travelled the world for countless years searching and searching for a way to join the human realm. He was weary and lonely and maddened by the relentless sun. As he sat panting in the dusty shade of an anthill, he wrapped his arms round his face and let out a long, despairing howl of defeat. He had finally accepted that it was not going to be possible. He would have to return to the core of the earth where he had originally come from.'

The Dream Dealer lit his cigar, taking a series of quick puffs to keep it alight. A rare smile of satisfaction spread across his face.

'I've often noticed that when you are at your lowest point – when you reach that moment when you give up and stop trying – then suddenly everything changes and things begin to happen.'

The little Earth-imp sunk her claw into his chest. She wasn't interested in his observations. She wanted him to get on with his story. The Dream Dealer winked at her and continued,

'Later that same day the earth-imp chanced upon a young boy who was on the eve of his initiation into manhood. The following morning, at sunrise, the boy had to set off alone into the bush to kill or be killed by a lion. The boy stood bravely before his tribal Elders but inside he was terrified. The earth-imp knew a way to ease fear, so, for his own amusement, he decided to

involve himself in the boy's experience. Little did he know that this boy held, not just the clue but, the actual key to becoming human.'

'Rubbish!' thought Finn.

'That night, as the boy dozed fretfully outside his village, a young girl crept out and lay down beside him. At first the earth-imp thought it was a lover but when he saw how similar they looked, he realised it must be the boy's twin sister. When they were finally sleeping, the earth-imp whispered in their ears that, beneath where they lay, they would find a magic root that would dispel all fear. The next morning the girl remembered, what she thought was her dream, and dug up the temor laxus root that the earth-imp had buried. She and her brother argued over whether it was right or wrong to eat it. The boy questioned whether he would be deceiving the Elders if he ate something that would stop him feeling afraid. Of course, he never thought that he might be deceiving himself, which was of far greater significance. Finally, in order to encourage her brother, the girl ate a piece of the root, and the boy soon followed her lead.

'Instantly, something appeared in the Jar. It was a red and yellow striped mist that gradually formed itself into a spiral. Then another spiral formed in the same colours and wound its way in the opposite direction.'

The little Earth-imp was so engrossed in the story that when the Dream Dealer took a puff from his cigar and then coughed she fell straight off his shoulder and onto the floor. She quickly scrambled back up and started scratching his neck for more. He enjoyed the luxury of sharing his experience with someone who could identify with every word of it. But it pleased him even more to be holding the attention of the boy.

'The earth-imp realised he was witnessing something of the utmost importance. And in an inspired moment thought, 'breath is the source of human life.' So he took off the lid and inhaled the striped helix. To his disappointment, nothing seemed to happen.'

The little Earth-imp was clenching her claws in anticipation.

'But as the girl was about to hurry back to the village, she suddenly looked across to where the earth-imp was sitting. She nudged her brother and pointed. They both stared in amazement. Of course, if they had not eaten the temor laxus they would have immediately run away from fear.'

'Why?' said Finn.

'Because they had never seen an earth-imp before. No human ever had.'

'Do all myths have a jar in them?'

'Stop interrupting and listen,' said the Dream Dealer, who was being assaulted by his irritable little companion. 'I'll answer your questions later.'

'Can you imagine the joy of realising he could be seen? Imagine that moment when the earth-imp knew he was at last in the human dimension of reality. Especially since he had given up all hope of it ever

happening. It is so obvious now but how could he possibly have guessed that he needed twins? Perfect male and female twins. Imagine his luck. And imagine the fury of Mother Nature, patient, passive and powerless to stop him.'

The Dream Dealer's lips curled in an amused smirk.

Finn shivered in the sun.

'I've got to go,' he stammered.

'Great story. One of my favourite myths,' said the Dream Dealer. 'Which reminds me, I found out something about your moth…'

But Finn had left. As soon as he had turned the corner he started to run.

*　　*　　*

'Slowly I'll tame him. Slowly, slowly,' said The Dream Dealer, gazing after him thoughtfully. 'Mother Nature's little pet. I've noticed how She's always watching him. Well, I want him too. I'd put money on his vapour being gold.'

He laughed an unearthly laugh.

The little Earth-imp turned her back on him and scowled. He stroked her gently, and said,

'We'll find twins for you, my little one. Trust me.'

The Earth-imp didn't trust him and she pinched him hard. She wanted to hear the end of the story because that always made her laugh.

'All right. All right. '*The sun rose and the boy set off with his spear into the bush. He was so out of himself after eating the root that, while he was skilfully tracking a large male lion, he failed to notice a pack of lionesses hunting him.*'

The little Earth-imp cackled with delight.

'So that's how I became human and he became dinner.'

The Photograph

One Sunday afternoon Finn was lying on the floor watching television. Hercules was sleeping and every now and then Finn would stroke him absentmindedly. Suddenly something woke the mouse. He slipped out of Finn's sleeve and set off purposefully across the room. Finn was absorbed in Cruft's Dog Show, watching the finals of the Shelties.

He had picked a dog called Mr Badger and when it won first prize, he clapped his hands. It was only then that he realised - Hercules was no longer up his sleeve. He searched the room but couldn't see his mouse anywhere. On his hands and knees he looked under the sofa and behind the television. As he was beginning to feel anxious he caught sight of the mouse running along the wall and disappearing behind the desk. Finn lay down and stretched his arm under the desk and felt around. His hand came across a pen, which he pulled out and put to one side. He then felt a thick piece of paper which he soon discovered was a photograph. At that minute Hercules ran out from under the desk and across the room towards the kitchen. Finn leapt up and raced after him. He caught the mouse and put him back up his sleeve.

The photograph was covered in fluff and dust. He wiped it on his trousers and studied it more carefully. The picture was of a group of people of different ages. There was an old man holding a baby, a couple with two girls, and his father, just recognisable, with a young woman and her baby sitting on a sofa. But it wasn't just any sofa. It was the same green patterned sofa that he had just searched under. So who was the woman? It had to be his mother. And the baby was obviously him. His heart thumped. He had a family.

Still staring at the photograph, Finn hurried into the kitchen.

'Dad. Look what I've found. Look at this picture. Is it you and …'

'Where did you find it?' asked Dad, a look of dread crossing his face as he glanced at the photograph.

'It was under the desk.'

'Why can't you mind your own business?' Dad shouted, unable to hide his panic. 'Who asked you to look under the desk anyhow? Give me that photo. Give it to me and get out of here.'

Finn held the photograph closely to him. He

stood there for a moment too shocked to move. Then he ran from the kitchen and out of the front door.

*   *   *

Dad sat down at the table and put his head in his hands. He had banished Finn's mother from his mind many years ago. He had deleted her from his life and he didn't need his son, or anyone else, to drag her back. It hurt thinking about her. He stayed like that, with the clock ticking and his head throbbing, until he could bear it no longer.

He went for the whiskey bottle in the cupboard, already knowing it was empty. He placed it on the table and looked around the room despairingly. He searched the pockets of his trousers and came up with £2.59. Driven by an urge he could not control, he went to Finn's bag, found his wallet, opened it and grabbed a £10 note.

Out of the dank tower block, and down the street to the Off Licence went Finn's dad – unaware that he was being followed by Flake, who had already noted Finn's departure. Hardly out of the shop, he pulled a half-bottle of whiskey from the brown paper bag and took a swig.

The Dinosaur Egg

The Dream Dealer had not seen Finn for days. He needed to know more about him. The more he knew the greater his influence would be. And it was going to take a lot of influence to capture Finn's soul.

'So, Flake. What's up?' asked the Dream Dealer, as Flake returned puffing to the Van.

'I'd say the f-father was into spirits,' answered Flake proudly.

'Ghosts?'

'N-no,' said Flake. 'This sort of spirits,' and he put his head back and glugged.

'Interesting,' mused the Dream Dealer thoughtfully. 'No mother, a father who drinks... should be the perfect candidate for us.'

The Dream Dealer handed Flake a bag of breadcrumbs.

'Now go and feed the birds. The boy's over there. Find out what's on that bit of paper he's carrying.'

'Feed the bbbbirds, Bbboss?' questioned Flake.

'He likes animals, right? So if you surround yourself with nice little dicky birds it will make him feel more comfortable, get it?'

*   *   *

Finn was mesmerised by the photograph. He looked and looked at his mother: it was his mother, it could only be. But the longer he looked the more distant she became. Her eyes couldn't see him staring at her. Her hands couldn't reach out and touch him. She sat there, silent, unfeeling, frozen in time. He sat on some builders' planks with the photograph resting on his knee, and imagined his mother walking across the road to tell him tea was ready and that it was time to come home.

Pigeons and sparrows had gathered round Flake as he stood a short distance from Finn, scattering crumbs onto the pavement.

'P-pleasant out here,' said Flake, glancing across at the photograph but not being able to make out any details. Finn opened his eyes, and when he saw Flake he closed them again.

'Don't be a bbbbully,' said Flake, shooing away a large, aggressive pigeon. 'Give the little ones a go.'

Finn opened his eyes and watched as a sparrow

landed on Flake's hand and sharply pecked up the crumbs. For a moment he forgot his own thoughts. Then the little bird attacked another sparrow as it attempted to steal some crumbs.

'The little 'uns are worse bbbbullies than the b-bigguns,' complained Flake to Finn. 'Did you see that?'

'Sparrows always fight,' commented Finn.

A gust of wind caught the edge of the photograph and flipped it over. Finn grabbed it before it blew away and returned it to his pocket. The Dream Dealer's eyes narrowed, as he watched from a distance. Nature didn't want him to see the picture.

'Hmm! Interesting. Wits about you, sonny,' he said to himself, as he walked towards his prey.

The birds rose in one big flock and flew noisily away. Finn watched them with surprise. He then noticed the Dream Dealer and froze. He had been trying to avoid him.

'The dinosaur egg's arrived,' said the Dream Dealer to Flake, deliberately ignoring Finn. He was carrying a parcel which he began to unwrap.

'That looks ancient, Bbbboss,' said Flake, as the Dream Dealer held up something which resembled a rough, old stone.

'A million years old,' said the Dream Dealer turning it over and examining it. 'Ever seen a dinosaur egg?' he continued, handing it to Finn. It was surprisingly heavy.

'Where did you get it?' Finn couldn't resist asking.

'I have friends – people who can find anything. D'you want it?'

'Why would you give it to me?' questioned Finn.

'I only bought it so I could see what one looked like. I'm not an expert on 'nature' like you.'

Finn felt confused. He was longing to keep the egg but he didn't want to owe this strange man anything.

'I'm not as *strange* as you think,' echoed the Dream Dealer eerily. 'I'm sensitive. Like I can see inside people. I can see your loneliness and your dad....I mean I don't like to say this but...does he have a bit of a problem with the bottle?'

'Shut up!' said Finn defensively. 'You don't even know him.'

'I don't know him but I do know what it is to have a dad who drinks. Mine did. I had to tiptoe round never knowing what mood he was going to be in. There were always secrets, things I couldn't talk about. I had to hold everything together. You know what I'm saying.'

Finn didn't answer and he didn't look at the Dream Dealer. But nor did he leave.

'Any news on your mother?'

Finn's hand tightened round the egg and then with a burst of will power he said,

'My mum's dead.'

'I don't think so,' murmured the Dream Dealer.

Finn tried to keep his voice steady but his heart was pounding with hope.

'What do you know?' he asked.

'Like I was telling you, my Ice-Dreams make you sensitive. You know things. You see things. You understand things. She's out there somewhere but you can't find her without me.'

Finn pushed the dinosaur egg into the Dream Dealer's hand and ran down the street.

*　　*　　*

'The bit of a paper? Is it a photo?' said the Dream Dealer to Flake.

'I think so, Bbbboss.'

'Of his mother, I expect.'

'I'm glad his mum's not dead, B-boss.'

'She may be for all I know – or care.'

Flake looking questioningly at the Dream Dealer.

'Don't worry yourself. Have a little Ice-Dream, Flake.'

'Th-th-thanks,' said Flake, hurrying to the Van.

'Curses!' cried the Dream Dealer, staring at his hands. The worm-like wrinkles were starting to form. He swore to himself as he strode towards the Van. The little Earth-imp was standing with the tube and mask at the ready. The Dream Dealer grabbed it and inhaled the coloured vapour from the Jar. When he had breathed in the required dose he turned to his accomplice and said,

'I'm bored of this ritual. I've got to put an end to it. I want that boy for my Jar. Watch me get him.'

Drink

Hercules's nose nuzzled the palm of Finn's hand. To Finn it felt like the only part of him that was alive. He didn't feel like going home. Yet he had to get away from the Dream Dealer. Every word that man said was disturbing. If the Dream Dealer knew that his father drank, then maybe he was right when he said that his mother was alive. Was it also true that he could help find her?

Everything felt heavy – from the fume-filled air to Finn's feet as he dragged them along the tarmac. Worst of all was entering the house. Every step felt as though he was walking against a force field. He wanted to get into his bedroom and shut the door but his dad called his name in the voice he dreaded. A voice made heavy by alcohol.

Finn pushed the photograph under a book and went into the kitchen. He forced himself to look at his father who was sitting at the table with his hand on a near empty bottle of whiskey. The ball in Finn's tummy burst with a wave of fury. He rushed to the table, grabbed the bottle and emptied the tawny liquid down the drain. He slammed the bottle on the side and stared defiantly at his dad.

'What the hell are you doing, Finn?' slurred Dad.

'What the hell are *you* doing? Get a life, can't you,' shouted Finn. 'Do you think I don't know that you sit here drinking while I am at school? Do you really think I believe you've got a job? I don't believe you even look for one. You kid yourself buying lottery tickets – wasting the little money we have. You're the biggest loser...'

Finn stopped as he heard what he had just said. There was a long silence when neither Dad nor Finn could look at each other.

'I'm sorry, Finn. I'm sorry,' Dad whispered.

But as he said it Finn noticed his wallet on the table. He picked it up and checked the money. £10 was missing.

'NO!' he screamed. 'You haven't taken my money again! Every time I nearly get there.'

Finn turned his back on his dad and stood with his fists clenched and his eyes squeezed shut, trying to block out the whole scene. A strange sound began to infiltrate Finn's space. At first Finn thought it was the cat that lived in the flat above but then, to his horror, he realised his dad was crying.

'I've failed you. I've failed myself…you'd be…'

'Stop feeling sorry for yourself,' spat out Finn.

'…you'd be better off without me,' sobbed Dad.

'Better off without you? That's rich! I haven't got a mother and you're suggesting I'd be better off without a dad, either. Thanks.'

'Finn. What can I do?'

'I don't know. Get help. Go to one of those places where they teach you to stop drinking.'

Finn paused. His anger had gone and his legs felt shaky. He went over to his dad.

'I need you, Dad. I need you,' he said, as his father put his arms round him and held him tightly. Together they wept.

The Birthday

Delphi's mum was making a cake. She wiped away a tear and sniffed. Then doing her best to sound cheerful, said to Delphi,

'What sort of icing do you want? Coffee, butter, chocolate, lemon…?

'Butter, I think. I hope Scorcher likes butter.'

'Very different party this year,' said Mum. 'Do you remember you used to insist on asking your whole class?'

'Course.'

'She's growing up,' said Delphi's step-dad, Mike.

'It's half-term break. People are doing other things,' said Delphi defensively.

She had asked Finn and Scorcher but Finn had said he wasn't free.

'Here's a little present,' said Mike, handing Delphi a round, untidily wrapped parcel. 'Apparently it came from Mexico.'

Delphi tore open the paper and took out a belt. It had brightly coloured stitching with a leather buckle. She held it round her jeans and her face changed from nervous suspicion to an approving grin.

'Thanks, Mike. I really like it.'

'I'm pleased,' said Mike, relieved to have made the right choice.

The doorbell rang and Delphi ran to answer it.

Scorcher was standing there with a long box, wrapped in silver and blue paper.

'Is that for me?' said Delphi, feeling quite excited. 'Come in. This is mum and this is Mike.'

Delphi had never seen Scorcher looking shy. It made him seem a whole lot younger.

'Nice to meet you, Scorcher,' said Delphi's mum, while Mike shook his hand.

'I'm Delphi's step-dad.'

Delphi looked at the long box.

'What have you got in there?'

'It's for your birthday,' said Scorcher quietly.

Delphi ripped off the paper and then began to tear at the cardboard box.

'It's a metal detector,' announced Scorcher. 'Not a kid's one, a real one. You can look for treasure.'

Delphi's mum let out a small cry and buried her face in the drying up cloth. Mike walked across the kitchen and put his arm round her. Scorcher looked at her in horror, wondering what he had said wrong.

'It finds coins and things, Mum,' said Delphi in an irritable voice.

'Let's go, Scorcher,' she continued, glaring at her mum and then indicating for Scorcher to follow her out.

Slamming the door, Delphi set off briskly down the street with Scorcher hurrying to keep pace with her.

'I'm really sorry. I don't understand what happened.'

'Nothing happened. I'm sick of all this. Come on, let's see how this metal detector works,' said Delphi, stopping and switching on the machine.

'You hold it just above the ground and then swing it from side to side. It makes little beeps and if it finds something it does one long beeeeeeeeeeep.'

'Sometimes I wish I'd never been born,' said Delphi, holding the metal detector in front of her and starting to walk. Much to Scorcher's relief they hadn't gone far when the machine started to make a beeping sound.

'Move it to the left. More. See, it's making a continuous sound. I wonder what we've found,' he said excitedly. 'It's something in the gutter. I'll have a look.'

Delphi stood and watched as Scorcher held up a twisted beer can.

'Must have been this.'

'Roman is it?' said Delphi sarcastically. 'We'll never find anything here.'

'Bet I will,' said Scorcher. But Delphi was already walking away. Once again Scorcher hurried after her.

'Delphi, I know what will cheer you up. Let's have an Ice-Dream.'

'That man's rubbish.'

'He makes good dreams, trust me.'

'I don't like him.'

'He's cool.'

The metal detector suddenly began to make a series of short beeps. Scorcher handed Delphi the machine and with their heads down they followed it as it led them into a side street. Neither noticed the Ice-cream Van, parked, waiting. The beeps grew more insistent until they became continuous. Delphi and Scorcher found their eyes resting on a black boot with red laces. They looked up to see who it belonged to and found themselves staring at their own reflections in the tinted glasses of the Dream Dealer. The three pairs of eyes together returned to the metal detector. The Dream Dealer lifted his foot and revealed a coin. Scorcher quickly picked it up and handed it to Delphi.

'An Australian dollar!' she said in disbelief.

'Wicked,' said Scorcher, turning to the Dream Dealer. 'She used to live in Sydney.'

'Great city. I've spent time there myself. I …'

'Maybe it's the dollar I lost at the beginning of term,' interrupted Delphi.

'I'll get you an Ice-Dream for your birthday.

What do you fancy?'

He looked questioningly at the Dream Dealer.

'What do you suggest – to cheer her up?'

'Depends what the problem is,' said the Dream Dealer, leaning back and observing Delphi. 'Parents playing up?'

Delphi's eyes widened and he realised he had hit the target.

'I never understand why parents grow so difficult when their children become teenagers?' he mused. 'They seem to get so moody and irritable and impossible to please. They become argumentative, secretive, tearful...'

'Why tearful?' Delphi butted in.

'Do they ever explain why they are tearful?' asked the Dream Dealer sympathetically.

'No, she won't tell me.'

'So how are you meant to help her?'

'I don't know.'

'It's very hard when you love someone – like your mum – and you want to help and yet she shuts you out. Pass me the mixing bowl, Flake.'

Flake had been leaning on the counter listening. He pulled a bowl from a shelf and handed it to his Boss. Then he reached for a basket full of sachets of powder with different names, hand-written, on them.

'Anything else, B-boss?'

'Thanks, Flake. Let's have a pinch of *Patience*, a

pinch of *Protection* – we don't want your feelings to get hurt,' said the Dream Dealer to Delphi, adding the powders into the bowl.

'We need a dash of *Wisdom*, and a speck of *Understanding*. What else do you think, Flake?'

Delphi's ears were ringing. She was no longer listening to what the Dream Dealer was saying. She was remembering the time Finn's dogs had run away and distracted her from taking an Ice-Dream. She remembered how tempted she had been to try one. She was remembering her mother warning her not to speak to strangers and never to follow the crowd. Then she remembered earlier in the afternoon when her mother had cried in front of Scorcher. She felt the anger rise in her. At that moment she decided she would definitely try an Ice-Dream. That would serve her mother right.

'And there we have a Floating Fireball,' came the Dream Dealer's voice. 'Happy birthday. Have it on me.'

Delphi reached out and took the sparkling scarlet Ice-Dream firmly in her hand.

'I'll have an Urban Wreck,' said Scorcher, handing Flake a £10 note.

Delphi took a large defiant lick, the chill slowly dispelling her anger. She and Scorcher went across to some steps and sat down silently concentrating on their Ice-Dreams. Gradually Delphi began to feel as if she was floating in a bubble. She felt light and carefree. She looked at Scorcher and smiled.

'Told you he was cool,' Scorcher said.

'Cooler than your metal detector,' said Delphi and they chuckled. The Dream Dealer watched them with satisfaction. What an inspiration his invention of Ice-Dreams had proved. Instant self-deception. The ultimate commodity.

'Nice to see k-kids laughing, B-boss,' said Flake ingratiatingly.

'Nice to see them hooked on happiness,' sneered the Dream Dealer.

Flake was about to say something but he thought better of it.

*   *   *

Suddenly the little Earth-imp leapt onto the counter and started beckoning urgently to the Dream Dealer. He immediately climbed into the Van and headed for the row of bottles. The little Earth-imp was cartwheeling with joy in front of the bottle with Delphi's name on it. The vapour had divided into gold and green stripes. She was a twin.

'GOLD! Exactly what I most want,' exclaimed the Dream Dealer. 'I don't even need to weigh it.'

The little Earth-imp had wrapped herself, like a piece of chewing gum, round the bottle and as the Dream Dealer's hand reached out, she clawed him so viciously that it drew blood. He laughed.

'I understand, my little one. You think it's for you because it's a twin. Sorry to disappoint you but half a twin is as good as no twin. I might as well put it in my Jar.'

The little Earth-imp leapt at the Dream Dealer's face.

'All right. Calm down,' he said, holding her firmly in his two hands. 'Tell me, what are the chances of finding the other one? Anyway, he or she's probably dead. But I won't touch Delphi's bottle. Promise. Scorcher will keep me going for now.'

Half Twins

T'he Dream Dealer was ripping open a box containing a new games console. He stood for a moment admiring its potential and then pushed it to one side. Kicking his boots through the white packing chips that lay scattered on the floor, he headed towards his private room.

In the far corner, the Earth-imp was struggling to attach the oxygen mask to the Jar. She was too occupied to notice the Dream Dealer enter. He stood for a moment watching her, a look of amusement and then pity flashed across his face.

'Look, my little one, I've told you a hundred times, the contents of this Jar are no use to you till you become human.'

The Earth-imp's head stretched into a sharp point and she gnashed her teeth.

'All right hu-woman. I haven't forgotten your twins.'

He picked her up and sat her in the palm of his hand.

'Don't sulk,' he said, looking at her scowling, scaley little face. 'You know how attractive I find it. Trust me, you're going to be a woman soon and then you'll be the foxiest little Earth-imp in the universe. The world's never been better. And I know –I've been in it for nearly two thousand years. It's our sort of world – and I've got it sussed.'

The little Earth-imp had forgotten her sulk and was listening enraptured.

'You don't want to be a celebrity or anyone famous – it's best to keep a low-profile. You just want to be the ordinary millionaire in the street,' expanded the Dream Dealer, enjoying sharing his observations. 'Life's about pleasure, fun, self-gratification and about never growing old. You and I will make hell on earth. Believe me it's a great century, in a great world.'

The Dream Dealer carefully placed the Earth-imp back on the shelf and then shouted for Flake.

'Time to weigh that twin. Come on, Flake, move it. Get the scales.'

'They're ready, B-boss,' said Flake, entering the room. 'And I've got the feather ready,' he added, trying to place the Dodo feather on one side of the scale but failing because it kept sticking to his finger.

'Give it here, moron,' snarled the Dream Dealer, pulling the feather deftly off Flake's sweaty hands and placing it on the scales. 'Now bring 'Jed' over here.'

Flake padded across to the shelf with the rows of neatly stored bottles and froze as he saw the one marked 'Jed' edging towards him. What he couldn't see was the little Earth-imp pushing it as hard as she could. He picked up the bottle and padded back to his boss.

The intensity of the Earth-imp's hopes and desires filled the room. Even Flake felt a nervous excitement as the Dream Dealer held the pink-and-blue-coloured bottle in the air.

'Cross your fingers. Cross everything,' he said.

The little Earth-imp immediately tied her legs and arms into a complicated knot while Flake crossed his fingers and his eyes. Then he lowered the bottle dramatically onto the scales and took his hand away. One side of the scales clanked heavily onto the table while the other side shot into the air with the Dodo feather bouncing lightly on it. The little Earth-imp buried her face in her hands in dismay.

'Brimstones. I hate wasting time,' roared the Dream Dealer, handing Flake the bottle and then giving him a hard push. Flake stumbled, hitting himself on a sharp corner of one of the shelves. The bottle smashed and the vapour sped in a trail of colour through the window returning swiftly to its owner.

'What d'you ddddo that for?' whined Flake.

'Because you're a moron,' explained the Dream Dealer.

'I was ggggoing to t-tell you something. Something I f-found out. Bbbbbut now I'm not ggggoing to t-tell....'

'I think you will, Flake. Particularly if it is something nice – something that will put me in a good mood and make me happy. You're such a good chap. I know how you like to make people happy.'

'I'm nnn-no-not going to t-tell you.'

'Yes you are, Flake. You know how pleased I will be with you.'

The Dream Dealer paused.

'Is it something about Finn?'

Flake eyes widened into complete circles.

'Ah, something about Finn. Now that does please me. Well done, Flake. So what did you discover?'

'His ddddad bought him a c-card.'

'A card. What sort of card? A Good Luck card? A Birthday card? A Get Well card?'

'It had a p-picture of a pppuppy on it.'

'Right. A puppy,' said the Dream Dealer flatly. He was clearly not impressed but he had been around long enough to know that even the most insignificant bits of information can often turn out to be of value.

From the corner of his eye he could see the Earth-imp pushing another bottle towards the edge of the shelf.

'Fetch me the bottle marked Delphi, there's a good man, Flake,' he said in a kind voice.

As expected, Delphi's bottle balanced exactly with the feather. The Earth-imp's eyes met the Dream Dealer's. She glared at him.

'She may be a twin and she may be 'perfect'. But as I've said, without the other half, she's no use to you,' said the Dream Dealer. The little Earth-imp squeezed herself into the shape of a tube and spat at him. 'I know how hard it is to find perfect twins,' he continued reassuringly. 'Of course we'll try to find the other half. Let's leave it on the shelf for now. Okay?'

Magical Sun

It was the sort of summer's afternoon that made you feel like lazing around. The air was hot and heavy. Flies buzzed about the discarded lunch boxes. Even Hercules wasn't moving. Finn was looking through half-closed eyes at Meg. She had missed morning lessons and was leaning against the school gates, gazing towards the Van. She used to be such a swot, now Ice-Dreams seemed to have taken the place of History lessons. Trixie was sitting with her back against the wall staring across the playground but seeing nothing. She no longer bothered to decorate her face with make-up and, though she was pale, Finn decided she looked almost bearable. He certainly preferred her indifference to her usual aggression. The kids seemed to be living in their own world, unaware of anything going on around them. Finn watched Scorcher come out of the building and stand blinking in the sunshine. He had just finished a detention for having missed his second art class. When Mr Turpentine had told him off, Scorcher had said,

'Either you can draw or you can't draw. Who needs to be taught art?'

Mr T. had gone off like a firework and made him write, 'I will not waste my talent', 300 times.

'How many did you write?' asked Finn, who had found the whole incident quite funny.

'10 and then lots of dittos,' answered Scorcher, clicking his fingers over and over again. It got on Finn's nerves. He stood up and moved away.

'You seem to have cheered up,' he said, noticing Abi laughing at Mr Turpentine gesturing in the distance. She had spent the whole of last week with large tears dropping onto the page of her Su Duko book.

'I have,' she said. 'I got Jed back.'

'Back from where? I've seen him around,' said Finn.

'Sure. He looked and spoke like Jed but it was as if the bit that makes him Jed was missing. It was horrible. I felt as if a part of me was dead.'

'And he's okay now?'

'Yeh. Yesterday, in English, he suddenly fell off his chair onto the floor, as if something had hit him in the chest. Smelly actually opened her eyes.'

'What had happened to him?'

'I don't know. She told him to get up at once and stop messing around. He did but he was blinking and looking all confused. He thought someone had hit him. Then he accused me of taking his pen. I just wanted to hug him. He was himself again.'

What of course they didn't know was that a few minutes earlier, Jed's 'self' had been sitting in a bottle on a shelf in the Dream Dealer's house. And worse still, if Flake had not broken the bottle, he might have lost it forever.

Finn noticed a group of boys who were kicking Cal's coloured football and asked if he could join them.

'S'pose so,' said one of the boys. 'Nobody else wants to be goally.'

Finn stood between the two shirts that had been placed on the ground. He managed to make a save and the ball bounced away, stopping against Scorcher's leg.

'Do you want a kick? We've got a match tomorrow,' said one of the boys.

Scorcher stared at him in a glazed sort of way and said, 'Good luck to you, man.'

'Save your breath,' said Finn to the boy.

'What's up with him – and the others?'

'They're into Ice-Dreams,' explained Finn. 'They should be called anaesthetic dreams. Watch this.'

Finn walked across to where Bela was sitting and tousled her curly hair. There was no reaction.

'I thought Ice-Dreams were meant to make your hair straight.'

'It's cool,' she answered.

'They're all so cool they'll find breathing too much effort soon,' muttered Finn, returning to the football.

'Delphi,' shouted Meg suddenly. 'Get me a Magical Sun.'

Finn forgot the game and looked over to the Van. He had noticed Delphi had missed the morning's classes.

'It's the l-last one,' Flake said, as he handed Delphi the Ice-Dream. 'They're very p-popular.'

'None left,' Delphi called back to Meg, as she took a lick from her sparkling Ice-Dream.

Meg's expression clouded over. She watched Delphi with narrowed eyes and followed her as she entered the playground.

'Give that to me,' she demanded aggressively.

'No way,' answered Delphi.

'Give it to me, now,' persisted Meg.

But Delphi held the Magical Sun just out of her reach. Meg jumped at it and knocked it onto the ground. The two girls, pushing and pinching each other, threw themselves onto the tarmac, fighting to get hold of the Ice-Dream. Delphi grabbed it first but Meg began hitting and kicking her. The boys stopped playing football and watched impassively. When Finn saw what was happening to Delphi he ran across and pulled Meg off, hanging on to her firmly until Delphi had walked a safe distance away. Meg struggled for a bit and then turned on Finn and spat out the word, 'Misfit,' before returning to her place by the school gates.

'Who's the misfit,' thought Finn. He walked across to Delphi. She glared at him and continued to pick out the bits of grit and dirt from her Ice-Dream.

'You okay?' asked Finn.

'Don't come lecturing me,' she replied.

'Can't you see what's happening to everyone?'

'Either join in or go away,' Delphi snapped.

Finn stood in silence staring at the ground. Delphi licked at her Magical Sun and felt the pleasant sensation of a bubble surrounding and protecting her. She let out a deep sigh as the fight with Meg faded away.

'Guess what? I got my final pound yesterday,' Finn said, pulling out his wallet and holding it in front of her. '60 quid!'

Delphi ignored him.

'There's something really important I've been wanting to tell you,' he continued, putting the wallet back in his pocket and pulling out the photograph.

'You already have,' said Delphi, closing her eyes with boredom.

'No. Something really important.'

'If you must.'

Delphi remained totally disinterested while

145

Finn described how Hercules had led him to the photograph.

'I think – in fact I'm pretty sure – it's a picture of my mother.'

'Nice,' she said in a flat voice.

'She's so beautiful,' he said, holding it in front of her face. But Delphi eyes were shut. She cared only about her Ice-Dream.

'Look. Look at it. I still can't believe it, Delphi,' he persisted.

'Don't believe anything. It's all just dreams.'

Finn felt he had been karate kicked in the stomach. Here was the most precious thing he possessed. He couldn't talk about it with his father. Delphi was the only person he wanted to share it with and she was totally uninterested. He stood up, his hurt turning to anger.

'I used to think you were different but you're no better than all the rest. Ever since you've got into Ice-Dreams, you're not Delphi anymore. You've changed!'

'Changed! Some of us have just grown-up,' said Delphi, finally showing some reaction. 'You're sad. Go and play with your pet mouse.'

Finn turned away, his eyes stinging and his chest feeling as if he had swallowed a stone.

The Yellow-Eyed Man

Delphi seated herself at a desk as far from Finn as she could find. The room was quiet except for the constant tapping of Scorcher's foot and the odd clap of distant thunder. Finn was watching the rain as it slid down the window. The drops hit the glass like tears and then raced each other to the bottom.

Miss Pelly opened her file and looked through her carefully typed pages. She noticed the silence and presumed her pupils were lost in creative thought.

'I have been putting together your ideas and we seem to have found a good background to our story. Would you like me to read it to you?'

Nobody answered.

'Good,' continued Miss Pelly. 'You can interrupt if anything doesn't make sense or you have a better idea.'

'*A young boy was driving his herd of goats up the slopes of Vesuvius. Suddenly the goats all stopped. He chucked some stones at them but they wouldn't move. They stood staring for a moment and then, with fear in their eyes, ran as fast as they could down the hill again. The boy was curious. He crouched behind a rock and watched as a small creature struggled out of a crack in the earth. The creature...*'

'Earth-imp,' said Finn firmly.

'Earth-imp?' queried Miss Pelly. 'All right then. '*The earth-imp had two legs, two arms, two small horns on his head and two piercing, yellow eyes. He was struggling with a large rock crystal jar that contained liquid gold. Even though the sun was shining, the gold glowed brightly with its own light. The boy had heard tales of these creatures. He knew that it meant the volcano was going to erupt and that many people would be killed.*'

'That's wrong. The boy couldn't see the earth-imp,' interrupted Finn. 'That's the whole point of my bit about the lion hunt. The earth-imp can't be seen till he finds the special twins.'

'Right,' said Miss Pelly, taking a pencil out of her hair and making a note.

Miss Pelly would never have guessed that Finn would become the authority on the story. But that was the exciting part of allowing children to use their imagination. You never knew which child was going to respond. It was, however, beginning to concern her that some of the children were not responding at all, not even to brownies.

Meg hummed tunelessly as Miss Pelly read on about how hard it is for an earth-imp to become human and how it can take place only when the creature is out of its own dimension. As she described the lion hunt, there was a flicker of interest from Cal who growled and pretended to be the lion before resting his head back on his desk.

'I'm going to tell you some bits from other myths I found because, I think, they help explain how the earth-imp evolved,' said Miss Pelly. 'Tell me what you think, Finn.'

'Can I tell you about my dream,' said Bela.

'Not now, thank you,' said Miss Pelly. 'Listen. Here's a bit that comes from southern China.'

'A band of oddities travelled from village to village. Crowds always gathered to stare at these strange aberrations of nature. There were Siamese twins with one head and four legs. There was a thread-man who was 8 foot tall and only weighed 5 stone. But the favourite was a semi-human creature with reptilian skin, claw-like nails, horns, carrying a …'

'…mouse called Hercules,' muttered Turk.

'…jar. Don't be silly, Turk,' said Miss Pelly sharply. 'The other thing that all the different stories seem to have in common is that this creature knows how to charm children.'

Scorcher drew a deep breath and giggled inappropriately.

'He wouldn't have got me.'

'Well, he might have done if he'd made you laugh,' suggested the teacher. 'Listen to this bit from a Mongolian legend describing how he cut through people's defences by making fun of them.'

If a grown-up was filled with self-importance, he would suddenly find, attached to his carved walking stick, the ugly creature with his chest puffed out like a pigeon in spring, his nostrils flaring and his features frozen with the disdain of someone who has just smelled a putrifying marmot dropping. The crowd recognised the parody and laughed, relieved that it was not directed at them. And the children, who lived in fear of grown-ups, laughed hardest of all. But by the end of each day the children had lost some of their liveliness while the creature seemed to have grown a tiny bit more human.'

'You mean the more children he tricks, the more he turns into a human. That makes sense,' said Finn, utterly absorbed.

'That is certainly what it sounds like. Humour was one means of his success but even greater than that was his exploitation of religion. Apparently, over the centuries he turned up in medieval Spain selling forgiveness from God to children who had been scared witless by their own priests. He appeared in peaceful Tibet encouraging revenge to those who had been wronged by their family and friends and there are even stories of him in Persia posing as a new prophet who promised eternal playtime for the children who gave their lives for his cause.

'By this time there was no longer any mention of horns or claws or scaley skin. He had become the man with the yellow eyes.'

'The man with the yellow eyes,' repeated Scorcher.

'We haven't said anything about, *Nature trembled angrily...*' said Finn, as a crash of thunder shook the window pane.

'Good. You can all think about that for next lesson. Then we must work on bringing the myth into our lives today.'

'I've got a bit, Miss,' said Trixie suddenly alert. 'I want to use those other words, *escaped Her control...*'

'Go on then, Trixie but get down off your desk, please.'

All the kids were thinking about something else, finally they had escaped her control, they were thinking about something else, they were in his control, in his control, in his control...'

Cal and Turk climbed on their desks and began chanting,

'*...in his control... in his control...in his control.*'

'Whose control?' shouted Miss Pelly. 'What are you talking about?'

The boys looked confused and slowly sat down again. Trixie began to cry. Miss Pelly handed her a tissue.

'If you can't behave yourselves we will have to do something less interesting.'

'Can I tell you about my dream,' repeated Bela.

'Not now, thank you Bela.'

'Man with yellow eyes,' said Meg. 'So where's he now?'

'I don't know any more than you do. The world's a big place, but I'm sure he's around somewhere,' answered the teacher. 'We must be alert.'

'Keep our eyes open, should we?' muttered Finn to himself.

Mr Turpentine
Notices Something

Finn sat by himself. He counted his £60 and tried to think about the puppies that were due to be born this week. It didn't cheer him up. He took out the photograph of his mother and stared at it. He looked at the baby in her arms and tried to imagine what it must have felt like. It hurt.

'Mum,' he said quietly. 'Mum,' he repeated, willing the face into life. 'Mum, I need you. Where are you? Answer me.'

But the face continued to stare out at him – lifeless, unchanging. He put the photograph back in his pocket and pulled out Hercules, glad to feel the warmth and life of his little mouse.

His thoughts turned to Delphi. Now he had lost her too. She was indifferent, uncaring and as unreachable as his mother in the photograph. A shiver passed through him. This was swiftly followed by a burning rage towards the Dream Dealer whose hateful Ice-Dreams had stolen Delphi from him.

Finn had called them anaesthetic dreams but sometimes they seemed to have the opposite effect. He hated this more. Over by the wall, Bela, Meg and Trixie were running in a circle round Delphi, shouting, 'Bye-bye blackbird,' over and over again.

Delphi was holding something. Finn wanted to know what it was. He moved a little closer. It was the nest he had showed her at the beginning of term. She was pulling it apart, twig by twig, and throwing the bits in the air. Finn was thankful the young birds had already flown, though he was pretty sure the blackbird had laid another lot of eggs.

The girls stopped running and stood in a line, with Delphi in the lead. She was shouting out orders, like an army officer.

'Enemy ahead. Grenades at the ready. FIRE!'

Finn watched in horror as each girl purposefully bent down and picked up a blackbird egg and smashed it as hard as they could against the wall.

'Hey, man. Can I hold that little rat of yours?' said a familiar voice.

Finn glanced briefly at Turk with his pale face and floppy hair and ignored him.

'He's cute. Give us a go,' persisted Turk. 'Come on, Hercules, it's good for you to explore another humanoid.'

Turk gently picked the mouse off Finn's arm and

watched wide-eyed as it ran up his sleeve.

Finn looked with contempt. He hadn't much liked Turk when he had bragged and bullied his way round the playground but now he hardly seemed a person at all. He was like the shell of a snail with the snail missing. Finn turned away and started counting his money again. After school he would go to Alf's house and see whether Alice's puppies had been born. He counted four ten-pounds notes, three five-pounds notes and the rest in loose change.

Turk had forgotten all about Hercules. Falling lightly to the ground, the mouse was now hurrying off in the direction of Mr Turpentine who was posturing outside the school building.

'How much money have you got there, Finn? You could buy loads of Ice-Dreams,' said Turk, who had begun to measure his life in terms of Ice-Dreams.

'Where's Hercules? What have you done with Hercules?' asked Finn, his voice rising with anxiety.

'Dunno. Must have run off.'

'What do you mean 'run off'? Which direction? Which direction did he run off in? He'll get trodden on,' cried Finn. 'Turk, at least help!'

But Turk wasn't even listening.

Finn got down on his hands and knees and looked along the ground. His ears were singing, his heart was beating and his head began to swim with the terrible fear that he had lost Hercules... forever.

The Playground seemed to grow silent. But

the silence wasn't just in Finn's imagination. The children had stopped talking. They were watching Mr Turpentine hopping about hysterically. He was frantically holding out his trousers and shaking his leg. But the more he shook his leg the harder Hercules clung on with his finely nailed little feet.

'Who let this wretched mouse out? Finn! FINN! Where are you? That will be 300 lines.'

Relief swept through Finn as he bounded across the tarmac. At that minute Hercules managed to scrabble his way up to Mr Turpentine's waist. Mr Turpentine had always been ticklish but this was unbearable. His body contorted like a rubber doll and he giggled and yelped and writhed and twisted until he caught sight of Finn and heard him saying,

'Thanks, Sir. Thanks so much, Mr T. I thought I'd lost him forever...'

Mr Turpentine grabbed Hercules as he crawled out of the top of his shirt.

'What d'you mean 'thanks, Sir'? Make it 500 lines. You can write, 'No mice up teacher's trousers' 500 times. Is that clear?'

'Yes, thank you so much. I'm so happy to find him'

'If you thank me once more for giving you lines – I won't give you any,' shouted Mr Turpentine, thrusting Hercules into Finn's waiting hands.

'Thanks, Sir,' said Finn, stroking Hercules who was twitching nervously.

'That's it,' screamed Mr Turpentine. 'NO LINES!'

'Great,' thought Finn.

* * *

Mr Turpentine was baffled. Why had he just told Finn he didn't have to write out any lines? And why were the children laughing at him? Out of the corner of his eye he could see Scorcher and Cal and also Trixie and Bela. They were standing nearby, staring into space. That was even stranger. Why were they not laughing at him?

'Finn, come here a minute.'

Finn followed Mr Turpentine to a quieter part of the playground.

'Look, old chap. What's going on round here? What's the matter with them?' he asked, pointing his head in Scorcher's direction. 'They're not themselves at all.'

'You've noticed, Sir.'

'We've just had a staff meeting. I'm told you're coming top in class and you're captain of football. Something's obviously very wrong.'

'Thanks a lot,' said Finn.

'No, no, no, no! Oh dear, you know what I mean.'

Finn nodded his head.

'It's not my fault, is it? You know, the children like this?'

'Course not.'

'You needn't be polite, Finn. I want the truth.'

'It's nothing to do with you,' said Finn. Mr Turpentine looked puzzled.

'Well, what is it to do with?'

'Ice-Dreams,' suggested Finn.

'Ice-creams. Really! Well, I always knew too many sweets weren't good for you but ice-creams...'

'Dreams,' interrupted Finn, 'Ice-Dreams. They eat them and then they don't seem to care about anything. They go all strange.'

The art teacher stared at the kids. He was struggling to make a connection. Sweets. Ice-Dreams. The kids. Himself. Where was the missing link?

'I'll visit the Ice-cream Van. See what I can find out. I am going to do something, Finn.'

The Splinter

The myth had worked its way into Finn's mind like a maggot into cheese. He couldn't get rid of it. The TV showed an earthquake in Pakistan, immediately Finn imagined Nature instructing one of her earth-imps to hurry with a jar of liquid gold to help the people who'd lost their families and homes. It annoyed him. It was a ridiculous made-up kid's story. It wasn't real. Yet something about it kept niggling. He didn't want to admit it to himself, let alone mention it to anyone else, but could there be the smallest possibility that the story was true? He had to know.

His chance had occurred in an unexpected way. Earlier in the week a splinter of wood had wedged its way under Finn's thumbnail. He had tried to squeeze it out but it wouldn't budge. He was still working on it when he left school and finally a little bit peeped out of the skin. If he hadn't bitten his nails, he could easily have pulled it out.

The Dream Dealer had noticed. He leapt across the street.

'Got a splinter?' he said, whipping a pair of tweezers out of his pocket.

Finn frowned. Hercules awoke and started scratching at his arm. Finn thought for a moment and then held out his thumb. Now it was the Dream Dealer's turn to hesitate. He couldn't see the splinter through his dark glasses.

'Sorry I can't bear to look,' said Finn, deliberately screwing up his face and turning away.

The Dream Dealer slid his glasses onto the top of his head and took hold of Finn's thumb. As he concentrated on capturing the splinter between his tweezers, Finn glanced up into his face. In that split second, he caught a glimpse of the Dream Dealer's eyes.

They were yellow.

The hair on Finn's arms and legs stood on end. His head seemed to separate from his body. The ground he stood on was no longer solid.

'You're shaking,' said the Dream Dealer suspiciously. 'I'm not going to hurt you.'

Hercules was shaking too.

'I'm just squeamish,' lied Finn, fighting his instinct to run away.

'Gone!'

The Dream Dealer flicked his dark glasses back on and triumphantly held up the splinter for Finn to see. 'Wasn't so bad, was it?'

'It didn't actually hurt at all.'

The initial shock had subsided and Finn, unable to stop himself, went on,

'You know that earth-imp in the story you told me? Did he ever manage to become human?'

There was a suffocating silence.

Finn could hear his heart thumping.

'You believe Cinderella's coach turned into a pumpkin, do you?' said the Dream Dealer coldly. 'Be careful not to mix fact with fiction. It's a sign of losing your mind. And people who lose their minds end up locked in an asylum. You wouldn't want that, would you?'

Finn shook his head.

The sound of traffic returned. A police siren wailed in the distance.

'Must rush. Forgot my homework.'

The Dream Dealer's golden eyes flashed behind their shades.

The boy knew.

Finn ran straight to the staff room and breathlessly asked to see Miss Pelly.

'Yes, Finn,' she said, her eyes firmly closed.

'It's all true. The Yewton Myth is true. The man selling Ice-creams is the earth-imp. He …'

Miss Pelly had opened her eyes and was looking

161

sternly at him.

'A myth is a means of telling a truth, Finn. That does not mean it is literally true. It is a metaphor. Is that clear?'

'But it is true, Miss. I saw his eyes. They are yellow.'

'So are my brother-in-law's. It probably means he has a bad liver. Probably drinks too much.'

'Please, please believe me. You've seen what the kids are like. You've heard them talking about the Dreams he sells them. If you don't believe me, go and see for yourself...you told us to look out for him. ... you...'

Miss Pelly had put her hand on Finn's forehead to see whether he had a temperature.

'You've been very creative in class but this is going too far. We're going to have to stick to grammar if you're going to be silly like this. Next lesson we'll do similes and metaphors.'

* * *

Finn found a pair of scissors and cut his 'Grammar for Dummies' book into a thousand pieces.

'Nobody listens. Nobody understands. Nobody cares. Mum, if you were here, you would believe me.'

Finn had gone to Alf. He knew Alf couldn't help him find his mother and he knew he wouldn't believe the story of earth-imps but Finn always felt better when he was with him.

'Alf, can somebody bad ever do anything good?' he asked.

Alf had chuckled and said,

'Sure they can. It's not what people do, it's *why* they do it. It's a bit like temptin' 'ercules with a bit a cheese and then catching 'im in a trap. Best avoid badduns.'

Alf was right. He must avoid the Dream Dealer.

The Ash Tree

Turk flicked the remains of his Ice-Dream cone onto the ground and smiled to himself. He was imagining sitting in one of Scorcher's squishy chairs with a bag of popcorn and the new computer game, 'Heroes of Crime'.

'Look! The Codemaster,' he announced with authority, pointing at Finn as he passed the Van. 'We've got to follow him to get to the next level.'

Cal licked the last bit of his Urban Surrender and entered the same bubble as Turk. Sure enough there, walking away, was the powerful Codemaster who would lead them through the maze of streets.

'He mustn't see us,' said Meg, as she joined the boys. 'If he turns round, we're dead.'

Finn was on his way to help Alf. He had no idea that he had become a central character in an imaginary computer game or that he was being silently stalked by a group of kids from his class. As he turned down a side street, the kids ran to the corner and Turk peered round.

'All clear,' he whispered. 'Keep quiet. If he sees us we lose power.'

They moved on, like a pack of hunting dogs, following their prey. Their eyes were focused so intently on Finn, that people walking down the pavement stepped onto the road to avoid them.

'First to put something in the post-box wins an extra life,' instructed Turk.

Tiffy instantly grabbed an empty cigarette packet from the gutter and raced to the letterbox.

'I've got the life,' she crowed, shoving the pack though the opening.

'Shhh!' said Meg, as the rest of the kids crowded round the box. 'The Codemaster mustn't know we're here.'

Keeping their distance, running then stopping, they followed Finn from one street to the next until they reached a housing estate.

'Wait,' whispered Turk. 'The Codemaster is about to enter a house.'

*   *   *

Alf was hurrying out as Finn arrived.

'I'll be back in a tick, got to get some milk. Keep an eye on Alice, me duk. She's started nesting.'

Finn's heart thumped excitedly. He rushed into the house, slamming the front door behind him. Digby chased round his legs, her tail wagging double-time at the thought of a walk. But Alice wasn't behaving like herself at all. Her tail was down and she was moving restlessly from place to place. Finn decided she was best left alone and headed for the garden, followed closely by Digby.

Suddenly the doorbell rang, long and insistently. Had Alf forgotten something? Finn hurried back through the kitchen but when he heard the sound of children's voices, he stopped. The bell rang again but Finn had no intention of opening the door.

There was a moment's silence. The children were whispering to each other. Then Delphi's voice called out,

'Finn. Finn. I need to tell you something. Something about the treasure.'

Finn was confused. He wanted to believe her.

'Open the door, Finn. Please. You're the only one I can trust.'

Finn's hand went to the photograph in his pocket and before he could stop himself he had opened the door. Delphi's trick had worked.

Like a river bursting its banks, the children surged past him, squashing him against the wall. Digby started barking.

'Get out of here, you idiots. Get out,' Finn shouted.

Nobody listened.

'The Codemaster's let us in,' called out Turk. 'We're on to the next level.'

Alice hid under the table and lay there growling.

'Look at the movie-clip. There's a pack of wolves. We've got to get past them and into the forest. Try the doors,' cried Cal, racing round the kitchen opening every cupboard and drawer he could find.

'It's this one,' shouted Trixie, opening the door onto the garden. 'Come on everyone. Follow me. I've found the way into the forest.'

Bela screamed.

Everyone stopped for a moment and looked at her.

'A vampire. Look. It's covered in blood,' she yelled, pointing at some tomato plants growing in a small glass shed.

'Get it! Get it!' shouted Scorcher, racing after her.

'It has to be pierced through the heart,' Turk shrieked, trampling through some blue irises and pulling a clematis off the wall.

Finn was standing with his hands clenched, watching helplessly as the children ravaged Alf's garden. Then he noticed Alice hiding under the table. He tried to call her out but she wouldn't move. He knelt down and carefully picked her up. She was trembling. He carried her into Alf's bathroom and locked the door from the outside. He then called Digby and shut her in the bedroom where she continued to bark as loud as she could.

'Get a stake,' shouted Cal, pointing at the ash tree. 'We've all got to get a stake.'

He wrenched a small limb off the tree and handed it to Turk. The other children gathered round and began pulling and tearing off the branches.

'It won't break,' said Meg, hanging onto a branch and swinging with her feet off the ground.

Scorcher added his weight until finally it snapped. Leaves lay scattered on the ground and soon all that was left of the tree was its mutilated trunk with some bits of peeling bark and a few jagged stumps where its young branches had once grown.

Next the children raised their weapons and rushed at the tomato plants. In a frenzy they smashed the glass and beat the plants to the ground, piercing and lashing the fruit to a red pulp.

'Level complete,' screamed Turk. 'Follow me.'

He raced back through the house and out into the street, followed by the others brandishing their branches and yelling wildly.

The colour had drained from Finn's face. As he went to close the front door, he found, like Alice, he was trembling. He stood for a minute with his back against the wall. He felt sick and his legs wouldn't support the weight of his body. He slid down onto the floor and closed his eyes, trying to shut out what he had just witnessed.

The key turned in the lock and Alf entered, his face full of concern. He had seen the gang of kids with their branches and known, instantly, where they had been. He hurried past Finn, through the vandalised kitchen, and into the trashed garden where he stopped abruptly, the breath knocked out of him. Every plant was lying broken on the ground. And his ash tree, which he had nurtured so tenderly, had been stripped, ravaged and destroyed. A few young leaves still shook and danced in the breeze but Alf knew his beloved tree had been sentenced to death.

Finn wandered into the garden and stood with his hand on the ash tree, unable to look at Alf.

'Is it going to be all right?' he asked.

Alf shook his head. He couldn't speak.

'I HATE them. I hate them with every bit of my being,' spat out Finn.

The sun continued to shine on the desecrated garden and somewhere a thrush was singing.

'It's not them, Finn. It's what they've done that's 'ateful,' answered Alf, with a catch in his voice.

Suddenly he turned to Finn.

'The dogs. What's 'appened to Alice and Digby?'

'I shut them up.'

'Well done, me duk,' said Alf, putting his arm round Finn.

Together they hurried back into the house.

Digby bounded out of the bedroom, bouncing and wagging as if nothing abnormal had happened. Finn unlocked the bathroom and Alf looked through the door. Alice had pulled his towel onto the floor and was lying on it. Finn and Alf could hear an unfamiliar high-pitched whimper. They looked at each other.

The first puppy had been born.

Delphi Wakes Up

Delphi lay on the bed in her room, staring at the broken ash branch on the table beside her. A shudder of shame passed through her. She turned the music up louder to drown out her thoughts. But nothing would stop them. Her mother knocked on the door and asked her to turn the sound down but she pretended not to hear. She lay there swearing furiously to herself.

She detested Mike. Last night he had banged his fist on the kitchen table and shouted at her. It was none of his business whether she was rude to Mum or not. Mum was hers. Mike wasn't even her dad, he had no right to tell her off. And Mum had taken his side and told her she wasn't allowed out this whole weekend.

Ever since her birthday everything had gone wrong. She wished she was back in Australia. She hated England. Nothing was fun anymore. School was boring, home was boring. She wanted to be with her friends but she even felt bored of them.

It used to be fun going to the market with Bela and Meg. They often found a cool top or piece of jewellery. But last time they went Bela had tried to steal an Indian skirt because she didn't have money. They had been chased down three streets and escaped being caught only by hiding behind a rubbish truck. Now Delphi didn't dare go back to the market in case someone recognised her.

She was fed up with Scorcher. She had asked him to share his fizzy lemonade, during break, and he had said 'no' and finished the whole can while she watched. She hated selfish people.

The only thing she looked forward to was Ice-Dreams. But thinking of Ice-Dreams made her think of Finn and that made her feel angriest of all. He was such a goody-goody. He had stopped her and Meg fighting over a Magical Sun. It was none of his business. Why couldn't he just leave her alone?

Then he had wanted to show her something boring, she couldn't remember what. And just because she wasn't interested, he said she had changed. Why did he have to say the most irritating thing he could think of? Who wants to be told they've changed? Changed into what anyway? He was the one who had changed. She didn't feel comfortable with him anymore. In fact she didn't want to be anywhere near him.

She remembered his face when she had told him to go away. He had looked all crumpled and pathetic. She couldn't stand that look. What was he trying to do? Make her feel guilty?

She got up from her bed and punched her duvet over and over again. She couldn't stand her feelings for one second longer. She had to get an Ice-Dream right now.

Delphi looked out of her window and saw her mum and Mike sitting outside the back of the house. She knew they were talking about her. Yesterday she'd heard her mother say they would be leaving soon because the school was doing her no good. She hoped they would go back to Australia.

Delphi left her music on full-blast, slipped out of her room and quietly left the house. It felt good to escape and to be able to channel her pent-up rage into big, angry strides. She heard the sound of the Ice-cream Van in the distance and she broke into a run.

There was a group of older kids gathered round the Van. She didn't want to get caught up with them so she remained at a distance and watched them buy Ice-Dreams from Flake.

'Delphi!' said a voice behind her.

She jumped. It was the Dream Dealer.

'Star of the playground. The one who shines brighter than all the rest. What can I get you?'

Now even the Dream Dealer irritated her. What did he mean by 'star of the playground'? He wanted her to buy a dream. Why didn't he just say so?

'Let me get you a Starry Surrender. Only a fiver. Cheap at the price.'

Delphi turned away. The Dream Dealer sensed her mood. He fetched an Ice-Dream and firmly put it in her hand. She held the Starry Surrender and then mechanically passed the Dream Dealer the money. She didn't speak and she didn't look at him.

He returned to the Van and pulled one of his expensive cigars out of his pocket and lit it with a long match. His hand was trembling impatiently but he still managed to puff out a perfect smoke ring and lasso his Jar. It wasn't quite full.

Delphi's anger had gone. She had got what she wanted – an Ice-Dream – and now she didn't want it anymore. She watched it melt and drip onto her hand and then onto the pavement. She closed her eyes in disgust.

All she could see was Finn. Finn, whom she had tried to shut out of her life. Finn, shining through the murk and mess that surrounded her. Finn's voice saying she had changed.

'I have changed. I am not who I was. I don't know what I think, or what I feel, or who I am.'

She remembered the fight with Meg and shuddered at the thought. How could they have physically fought? She had never done that in her life before, let alone over an Ice-Dream. And hadn't Finn been trying to protect her from Meg?

Why had she been so mean to him? Why didn't she care that he had finally got his £60? Why didn't she want to see whatever it was he wanted to show her so badly? How could she have been so hurtful and heartless?

She felt sick.

She flung the Ice-Dream onto the street.

She wanted to have a shower and wash away the sticky mess and all the confusion of the past few weeks. She wanted to be hugged by her mother. But most of all she wanted to say sorry to Finn.

A rubbish lorry was noisily crunching the contents of the street's bins but Delphi heard only the lilting trills of a blackbird. 'Birds with suitcases', she whispered and ran towards home.

* * *

As Delphi had thrown away the Ice-Dream, the Dream Dealer had winced.

'I don't like that girl.'

'At l-least you ggggot the money off her,' tried Flake.

The Dream Dealer looked at him witheringly.

Flake nervously started counting the money out of the till.

'You've made some serious mmmoney. More than

any ordinary ice-cccream seller, I bbbbet.'

'How much do you bet, Flake? A thousand pounds? A million pounds?' sneered the Dream Dealer.

Flake hung his head, wishing he had kept his mouth shut.

'Of course I love everything that money can buy. That's why I chose to become human,' barked the Dream Dealer.

'Human, Bbbboss? I don't understand.'

'That's what I love about you, Flake. You don't understand anything, do you?'

'N-no, Bbbb...'

'... and I'll tell you something else you don't understand,' continued the Dream Dealer, talking more to himself than Flake. 'You humans need meaning in your lives. Even I get the odd little twinge. The desires of a human heart just aren't satisfied by a fat bank account.'

'Yes, B-boss.'

The Dream Dealer glared at Flake.

'I mean, nnnnno, B-boss.'

'I dreamt of being human but it isn't enough. Human or not, if I've got to die, I'm no better than this cigar. Alight one moment...'

He took a puff and watched the tobacco crackle and glow.

'...and a pile of ashes the next.'

The Dream Dealer tapped the ash from the end of the cigar onto the floor and kicked it with his boot.

'And as long as everything ends in death, then Mother Nature remains boss.'

Flake looked at the ground. He was sure he had felt it shake.

'Why have you got it in for Nature?'

'Because she's too powerful,' answered the Dream Dealer unpleasantly. 'But luckily she has a fatal flaw. She has to obey her own laws. And her laws dictate that everything in the universe has to live according to its own intrinsic nature. A tiger can never become a vegetarian anymore than you could become a bumble bee, Flake.'

The Dream Dealer picked up his precious Jar and stroked it.

'But you, my beautiful, have helped me break nearly all Her laws. Only one, final step left and we've got to be quick. A dash of gold perhaps and the alchemy can begin.'

'And then wwwwhat?'

'I'll live forever and ever and ever and ever. Then I really will be boss,' rasped the Dream Dealer, narrowing his viper-like eyes.

The sun was sinking behind the high-rise buildings in an orange and brown haze of pollution. A sudden squall whipped up the dust and sent some red-hot ash into his face.

'Ow! Temper, temper. She's angry. Very angry,' smirked the Dream Dealer, rubbing his cheek.

Flake's eyes widened in horror.

'Oh cheer up. Give yourself an Ice-Dream,' said the Dream Dealer recovering himself.

Flake reached for an Ice but then hesitated. Deliberately he whispered to himself, 'No!'

A Dream That Will Last

A miserable looking figure was heading for the Van. Scorcher stopped and wrapped his arms across his chest as if he were cold. He hadn't been to school for days. He was staring at the ground but seeing nothing. Three words were rotating through his mind. 'Who am I? Who am I?' It was as if the colour had drained from the world. All was grey and flat and empty. The only feeling left in him was fear. Fear of dying, fear of living. 'Who, who, who, who, am I, I, I, I, I...?'

'You need a dream,' spoke the Dream Dealer softly into Scorcher's ear.

'I need a dream,' repeated Scorcher.

'A dream that will last.'

'A dream that will last,' echoed Scorcher. 'Yes, I don't want to wake up from it, like all the other times. One that will last.'

The Dream Dealer walked round and stood in front of Scorcher.

'I have the perfect dream for you. A dream that will last. A dream that you won't wake up from. But it's expensive. Very expensive.'

Scorcher looked up desperately into the face of his saviour.

'Give it to me. Give it to me. How much? I'll pay anything.'

'You've always got money, Scorcher, haven't you? Well, this time it's £75.'

Flake gasped. The Dream Dealer turned to him and smiled sweetly.

'Giving has to be a sacrifice if it's going to mean anything.'

Then he whispered to himself,

'And – the bigger the sacrifice the fuller my Jar.'

'Seventy-five pounds!' exclaimed Scorcher.

'If you really want it, you'll get it. I trust you.'

'But I've given you all my money,' shouted Scorcher, his voice rising in panic. 'I haven't got any left.'

'Don't get all upset. We'll come to some arrangement. What do you think, Flake? Shall we let our friend here have it for SIXTY POUNDS.'

Flake squirmed uncomfortably. He opened his mouth, trying to form the word, 'no'.

'Flake, what do you think?' persisted the Dream Dealer.

'You're the boss, B-boss,' he muttered weakly.

'All right. All right. Sixty pounds. I'll get it. I'll get it somehow,' said Scorcher shuffling away.

The Dream Dealer's lips curled into a smile. His plan was developing nicely.

Finn's Money

Finn raced into the locker room and tore open his bag. Some books and paper spilled onto the floor. He pushed them back and yanked out his wallet. He quickly tipped some change into his hand, put the wallet back and half threw the bag into the locker. He then sped down the passage to the pay phone and hurriedly dialled a number.

'Hi Alf,' he panted. 'What's happening? How's the little runt?'

He listened to the reply, his face tense.

'Is it feeding okay?'

His eyes sparkled as Alf described the scene.

'Can I come and see it now?…Not today?… Is something wrong with it?…Okay, I'll come tomorrow.'

Finn left the telephone box, a smile still on his face, thinking only of his puppy. He had noticed Delphi in the distance. She was the last person he wanted to meet. He darted into an empty classroom and sat with his back against the wall. Hercules crawled out of his sleeve. Finn placed him on his knee and they stared at each other.

'Hercules,' whispered Finn, 'my little puppy's not very strong. I really, really, really, really hope it's going to be okay.'

Hercules jumped off Finn's knee, onto his chest and ran up to his neck. Finn caught him and held him in his two hands. He couldn't bear it if the puppy died. He hadn't even seen it yet. It had to live. It had to. Life couldn't be that unfair, could it? He closed his eyes and immediately saw the face of the Dream Dealer.

He quickly opened them again and focused on Hercules' twitching whiskers. He was thinking of the photo of his mum and the Dream Dealer's words: 'You won't find her without me.'

'Hercules, I've got to find mum. You'll help me find some clue. You'll help me find her, like you found the photo, won't you?' begged Finn.

He was struggling to shut the Dream Dealer out of his mind.

* * *

Scorcher was also on a mission. He had to get hold of £60. At that moment, it was as important to him as it was for Finn to find his mother. Scorcher knew there was only one person in the school who would have £60 in their bag and he knew where to look.

He headed for the locker room and leant against the wall. The room spun round him. The lockers kept coming in and out of focus. He forced himself forward, down the row until he found Finn's locker, which was above his own. It was open. 'A dream that will last,' he muttered, as he grabbed the bag. The idea that he might be doing something wrong never entered his head.

Finn's Dream

The puppy had died that night. Finn never even saw it. He hadn't spoken to anyone, not even Hercules, in the last twenty-four hours. He didn't trust his voice not to crack. Alf had promised that when Digby had puppies Finn could have one, even if there wasn't a runt. Nothing cheered him up. The hole inside him felt so big that if he fell into it, he would never climb out.

'I know where she is,' said the familiar voice in his head. 'Only I can help you.'

Finn was being drawn to the dark figure, like a moth to a light bulb. He knew it was wrong. He knew it was dangerous. And he knew it was inevitable.

'It's your fault, mum. If you were here, I wouldn't have to do this.'

Finn slipped unnoticed across the Playground and into the street. Flake was helping some children to Ice-Dreams. Standing in the shadow of a tree was the Dream Dealer. He was waiting for him.

'Have you found out anything?' Finn asked, without bothering to say hello. 'You told me you had friends who searched for lost people? Have you found her?'

'I'm glad to report there is progress,' answered the Dream Dealer convincingly. 'But I need your input. As you rightly said when we first met – this is about YOUR dream.'

Finn looked imploringly at the Dream Dealer.

'But I don't know anything. I've searched every drawer at home. There's nothing.'

'Nothing?' questioned the Dream Dealer. 'What about your photo?'

Finn was intrigued.

'Of your mum and...?

'...Mum and Dad and me... as a baby,' Finn continued automatically.

'And...?'

'...and two little girls and an old man and another baby and ...'

'Another baby!'

Little did Finn know how the Dream Dealer's mind was racing and making connections. Was Finn a twin? The card with the puppy. A birthday card. Delphi's birthday. Delphi a twin. A pair of perfect twins...

'It's a picture of my family,' explained Finn.

'Just had a birthday, have you?' said the Dream Dealer.

'How do you know?'

'It's a sixth sense I have. You have a sixth sense too but it's not very developed.'

Finn looked doubtful.

'Surely you know about the Super Natural. It's a force much greater than Nature. Nature won't be boss for ever,' gloated the Dream Dealer.

Finn felt the hair rise on the back of his neck.

'I don't think a sixth sense is supernatural, it's normal,' he argued. 'It's natural in birds, it's natural in animals, so why shouldn't it be natural in humans?'

Finn had often noticed how Alice and Digby knew when Alf was coming home. They waited by the front door for at least five minutes before he arrived.

'That's because humans don't need a sixth sense anymore,' reasoned the Dream Dealer. 'They have mobile telephones, and machines to tell them what the weather is going to be. Their sixth sense has withered away like the tails they used to have.'

Finn could not argue with this. He stood silently as the Dream Dealer continued persuasively,

'You see it's not me that holds the key to finding your mother. It's you.'

'But how?' asked Finn, trying not to show his desperation.

'I've told you before.'

'You're not on about Ice-Dreams again?'

'They're the only way to enhance your sixth sense,' stated the Dream Dealer, turning away as if he were bored by the conversation.

Instantly his body tightened and his nostrils flared.

'Turpentine. Change the sign. I smell Turpentine.'

'I've bbbbeen painting the Van, do you l-like the colours?' asked Flake, pointing at the Van with a shaking finger.

'Turpentine the teacher – you miserable moron,' spat out the Dream Dealer, as he swiftly changed the D to a C and melted away into the lane behind the Van.

Finn frowned as he saw Mr Turpentine come tiptoeing out of the school gates.

'Ah ice-creams!' said Mr Turpentine in an exaggerated way.

Finn wished he would just act normally instead of pretending he was some private detective.

'Fancy a nice, ice-cream, eh?' he added, winking meaningfully at Finn.

It was embarrassing. Finn couldn't bear to watch. He turned his back and started talking to Hercules.

* * *

Flake deliberately picked up the crystal Jar and bravely stood it on the counter.

'What's that?' asked Mr Turpentine looking

puzzled. 'Beautiful colours. I'm sure I've seen that somewhere before.'

But the harder he tried to remember, the further away the memory went.

'B-ben?' whispered Flake.

His eyes darted nervously as he saw the Dream Dealer approaching. He quickly hid the Jar again.

Mr Turpentine stared at the large, stuttering figure. Suddenly a complete scene flooded before his eyes.

He was 13. He was painting a mural on a wall – commissioned by Yewton Town Council. His best friend, Fred Lake, was helping him mix the paint. Down the street was a magician, in a top hat, performing fantastic tricks. School scarves were changing colour and doves were appearing from behind children's ears. The magician was offering him magic sweets. They would make him a famous painter, instantly. He bought a whole bag of sweets ...

'Good afternoon, Mr Turpentine,' came the charming voice of the Dream Dealer. 'Come to admire the Van? Flake's been painting it. Talented, isn't he?'

'Very talented, I wish he was one of my pupils,' answered Mr Turpentine, trying to sound calm and in control.

'I'd love to be one of your p-pupils. I'd gggg...'

'Shut up, Flake!' snapped the Dream Dealer.

Finn turned to the Van. There was something about

it he hadn't noticed before. If you looked carefully the design became a spider's web and in the top corner Flake had painted a predatory yellow-eyed spider. Finn glanced at Flake and then at the Dream Dealer.

'Are we flies being drawn into the trap?' he asked.

The Dream Dealer leapt between the Van and Mr Turpentine,

'Quite the naturalist, this boy. If it's not mice or dogs then it's flies. Isn't that right, Mr Turpentine?'

The art teacher nodded inanely.

'Can I get you an ice-cream? I'm sure you've had a hard day,' continued the Dream Dealer soothingly.

'Thank you, I will. With a flake please, Flake.'

Mr Turpentine giggled nervously. A look of distaste passed over the Dream Dealer's face.

'Good one, Mr Turpentine. Stick a flake in it, Flake,' he said, forcing out a polite laugh. 'And make another one for this boy here. Put away your money. You can have them on me.'

'That's very kind. Very kind indeed,' said Mr Turpentine, looking at Finn for reassurance. Neither noticed the Dream Dealer swiftly swapping the ice-creams for Ice-Dreams.

'Here, my friends, try these. Mr Turpentine, take this. Finn…'

'No thanks.'

'No thanks?' questioned Mr Turpentine, taking an Ice-Dream in each hand and licking first one and then the other. 'Delicious!'

Mr T. was experiencing the warm glow of an enveloping bubble. He quickly forgot his reason for visiting the Van.

'Excellent ice-creams.'

'Why don't you tell Mr Turpentine about Ice-Dreams?' asked Finn, turning to the Dream Dealer. 'Go on tell him.'

The Dream Dealer rocked back on his heels and laughed uproariously.

'Dreams! How can anyone sell dreams?'

He continued laughing and patting Mr Turpentine on the back until he too joined in the joke. The Dream Dealer then turned to Finn and whispered fiercely,

'If you want to see you mother again – alive – you'd better keep your mouth shut.'

Mr Turpentine was beginning to feel a little queasy. He sat himself down with his back against a tree and closed his eyes.

Fred was passing him a rag to wipe his brush on – the rag had blues and purples and yellows and oranges swirling on it – it was a Jar – a Jar standing on the Magician's table – a Jar – an ice-cream – ice-cream ...

'Are you all right. Mr Turpentine?'

Mr Turpentine opened his eyes and saw Finn leaning over him.

'Just having a little doze. Having a little dream. Remembering a little something. Can't quite get it...'

'Do you feel okay?' continued Finn, helping

Mr Turpentine to his feet.

'I feel good – or maybe – strange…'

'Like what?' questioned Finn. 'Like you've got a sixth sense?'

'Maybe a sixth sense– or maybe no sense or nonsense or…'

Mr T. grabbed Finn's arm. He was having difficulty balancing.

*　　*　　*

Finn clenched his fists in frustration. He felt like his head would split in two.

'What do I do?' he thought. 'What should I do? I know Ice-Dreams are wrong and I know they're bad but it is the only hope I've got – the only possible solution – what do I do?'

'Go for it. Whatever it is you want, Finn. Go for it,' said Mr Turpentine firmly.

Finn froze. Mr Turpentine had answered the question in his mind. Had the Ice-Dream really given Mr T. a sixth sense? Could his own sixth sense find his mother as the Dream Dealer promised?

Immortality

T' he Dream Dealer tickled the little Earth-imp under the chin. She could feel the nervous tension emanating from his finger. The vapour in the Jar was a hair's breadth away from reaching the minutely engraved eternity symbol. And how right she had been to hang on to Delphi's bottle.

'Everything to gain, my little one. We'll get Finn's soul for you and…'

They both looked towards the school. A forlorn figure was approaching.

'… and I'm almost certain Scorcher will be enough for me.'

Scorcher was dragging Finn's bag. As he reached the Van he pulled out the wallet and waved it.

'60 quid. I've got it. Here's 60 quid.'

The Dream Dealer walked round the Van and patted Scorcher on the back.

'I knew you'd do it. Such determination. You'll go a long way. A very long way.'

The Earth-imp sniggered. The Dream Dealer emptied the contents of the wallet into his pocket and threw it onto the ground. He then removed the photo of Finn's mum from the bag.

Flake hung his head.

'Now Flake, what did we promise Scorcher here? The Almighty Wondrous Paradise Dream. Isn't that right?'

'Bbbbe cc-ca-careful of him, B-boss.'

The Dream Dealer reached over the counter and picked up the biggest, brightest Ice-Dream of all. Scorcher grabbed it and took a bite. The colour seemed to drain out of the boy. He appeared almost like a sepia photograph. The Earth-imp was watching the Jar. The vapour rose to the lid and began to fizzle and froth.

'Sweet dreams,' hissed the Dream Dealer.

* * *

Scorcher was inside his bubble. The sky was a pale turquoise and a golden egg was floating across it. A planet spun past, showering diamonds into space. Scorcher laughed but the laughter caught in his throat. The skin of the bubble was thick, like rubber. He could hardly breath. The bubble burst and the rubber filled his mouth and nose. He fell to the ground.

Flake stood paralysed. His eyes were on Scorcher but his feet didn't move. The Dream Dealer didn't like what was happening to Flake. There were signs that feelings had once again begun to flow through his veins. He was like a huge iceberg that had begun to thaw. Drip, drip, drip.

The little Earth-imp was scratching madly at the Dream Dealer's hands, frantic to get his attention. He looked at her and for the first time there was a look of compassion in his strange yellow eyes. He knew what she was thinking. Once he had achieved what he wanted he might forget about her, and she was helpless without him.

'I won't desert you, my love,' he said. 'What is the point of my becoming eternally human if you can't be a hu-woman with me?'

He wanted someone who understood where he came from and who could share the joys of the darker side of human life.

The Dream Dealer's dream was about to be realised. The vapour in the Jar was changing from a swirl of varying colours to an intense blue. It was only a matter of minutes until the vapour had passed through all the colours of the spectrum and then it would be ready to inhale.

The Dream Dealer was on the verge of immortality. But something else was transforming, not just in the Jar, but in the Dream Dealer himself. For the first time he was thinking of someone beyond himself.

He could actually feel the Earth-imp's desperation. Her longing to be human was almost more important to him than his own desire to become immortal.

He had to get Finn fast. Time was running out.

A group of kids were heading out of the school gates towards him. Cal was in the lead. His eyes were focused hungrily on the Van. He almost fell as he tripped over the body of Scorcher. It might as well have been a paving stone for all he cared. Neither he, nor any of the other kids following him, gave the body a second glance.

They reached the Van and started banging aggressively on its side, demanding Ice-Dreams. The Van shook and so did Flake. His eyes were darting uncomfortably from Scorcher to the children and then to the Dream Dealer.

'Quick, Flake. Ice-Dreams. Don't worry about money. Give them anything they want,' ordered the Dream Dealer, looking over Flake's shoulder. 'Relax kids, there's plenty for everyone.'

The children pushed and jostled and argued as they fought to get an Ice-Dream.

Flake shelled them out reluctantly, but fast, under the gimlet eye of the Dream Dealer. Gradually the children became enveloped in their bubbles again and a calmness settled over them.

The little Earth-imp was leaping and cart-wheeling on the roof of the Van. She could see Finn in the distance. Here was her hope, her dream, her human life-giver. It was clear by the way he was walking that he had finally decided to try an Ice-Dream.

Scorcher's Nightmare

T'he Dream Dealer had seen Finn too. He pushed his way through the throng of contented children and arrived, casually, in front of the boy.

Finn reached automatically in his pocket for the reassuring warmth of Hercules. Then he remembered his decision to leave Hercules at home. His mouse had made it quite plain what he felt about the Dream Dealer. Finn had to go through with this alone.

'Okay. I've decided,' said Finn, before the Dream Dealer had a chance to say anything.

'To let me help you?'

'Yes,' said Finn, his fists clenched as if he was forcing himself.

'My pleasure,' purred the Dream Dealer. 'I feel your mother isn't all that far from here but I can't get more information. Only your own sixth sense can lead you to her.'

Finn nodded.

'FLAKE!' shouted the Dream Dealer unnecessarily loudly. 'Finn would like to have the Mother-Dream.'

Flake was desperate. As his boss looked away, he deliberately picked up the wallet that Scorcher had stolen and placed it on the counter in front of Finn.

'The Mmmmother-Dream, right you are, B-boss,' he said.

'Mother-Dream,' repeated Finn.

Flake nudged the wallet. It caught Finn's attention.

'What's this? Who took this?' he asked, looking inside. 'My £60. Who the hell's taken my £60?'

'Sss-cccor…' stuttered Flake.

'Get the Dream,' hissed the Dream Dealer to Flake. 'You're in big trouble.'

Finn's tension turned to blinding fury.

'Scorcher, where are you? Just wait till I get you.'

The Dream Dealer stepped closely in front of him.

'You've more important things, Finn. And little time.'

'I'll kill him,' yelled Finn, pushing past the Dream Dealer.

'I'm leaving soon,' threatened the Dream Dealer. 'And if I leave you'll never find your mother.'

He reached over the counter, took the Mother-Dream from Flake and held it out to Finn.

'Now concentrate,' he said, as Finn slowly took the Ice-Dream from him. 'You'll see your mother…'

'My mother,' repeated Finn, holding the Ice and staring at the Dream Dealer.

'You must ask her where she is.'

'Where she is,' echoed Finn.

'Now lick the Mother-Ice D....'

An agonised scream sliced the air, breaking the spell. It came from Scorcher.

*   *   *

Scorcher's eyes were shut but he was making sweeping gestures with his hands and writhing around feverishly. All he could see were spiders. Spiders crawling up his arms, down his neck, into his ears, up his nostrils. A huge spider, with the face of his mother was caressing and suffocating him. And then an even larger spider, with the piercing yellow eyes of the Dream Dealer, was spinning a web round and round him till he couldn't move, couldn't even open his mouth. He fell back onto the ground, silent and still.

*   *   *

Nature was watching. Was this the moment She had been waiting for?

For a split second Finn looked longingly at the Mother-Ice-Dream and then he dropped it on the ground and ran to Scorcher. He knelt down beside the still figure and put his hand on the boy's shoulder.

'Wake up. It's me – Finn. Open your eyes.'

Scorcher's eyelids flickered. He grabbed Finn's arm and held it tightly. Finn looked at the half-eaten Ice-Dream lying on the ground beside him and then accusingly at the Dream Dealer.

'What have you done to him? Is he going to die?'

The Dream Dealer said nothing. He could not believe that Finn had chosen to put the wellbeing of Scorcher before the one thing he most wanted in the world.

'Don't just stand there,' shouted Finn to the other children. 'Turk, Meg, someone – GET HELP!'

But it was useless. Nobody moved. The kids stared and Flake stood frozen. The Dream Dealer slowly picked up the Mother Ice-Dream and came towards Finn.

Finn grabbed Scorcher's mobile telephone and switched it on.

'Don't throw your dream away,' coaxed the Dream Dealer. 'Don't throw your mother away. Don't you love her anymore?'

'I'm calling the police,' answered Finn firmly.

'I wouldn't try that…' said the Dream Dealer, '… not after what you've done to Scorcher.'

He kicked the mobile with the tip of his boot and sent it spinning under a car.

'He stole your wallet and you decided to do him in, did you? A bit harsh, wasn't it?'

'What?' said Finn, unable to believe what he was hearing.

'You killed Scorcher. He killed Scorcher, didn't he kids?'

'He killed Scorcher,' repeated the kids in one voice.

'Got him by the neck, like a rottweiler. Saw it with my own eyes. Isn't that right?'

'He killed Scorcher,' continued the kids.

'He's not dead …' shouted Finn, looking with disgust at the Dream Dealer's hands as they began to shrivel and grow leathery.

'Murderer,' growled the Dream Dealer. 'Shall we punish him?'

'Punish him,' repeated the children.

'Shall I destroy his precious dream?'

'Destroy his precious dream,' chanted the children.

The Dream Dealer pulled the photograph of Finn's mother out of his pocket.

'Don't touch my mother,' shouted Finn.

'I'll do a deal. You eat the Ice and I'll give this back to you.'

'Keep your poisonous Ice-Dreams.'

'So it's bye-bye to Mummy, is it?' sneered the Dream Dealer, holding up the photograph. Slowly and deliberately he ripped it into little pieces.

They fell like snow around Finn's head.

Finn leapt to his feet and, though his eyes were blurred by tears, he lunged at the Dream Dealer.

The Dream Dealer stepped to one side with the elegance of a bull-fighter. Finn fell forward, hitting his head on the side of the Van. He lay on the ground, stunned.

Time To Move On

The wrinkles in the Dream Dealer's neck were beginning to creep up his face, transforming him from man to monster. His piercing golden eyes were darting from side to side, weighing up the situation. Two children's bodies lay on the ground. It was time to leave. He had lost the battle for Finn's soul and the humanisation of his little Earth-imp, but he would find other perfect twins, somewhere – someday. He, of course, had all the time in the world. His Jar was waiting ready for him to inhale. He had done it even without gold vapour. Immortality was guaranteed.

'In the Van, Flake. Start the engine. We're off.'

Flake was staring at the shrivelling, shrinking figure before him. The de-humanisation of his Boss was more terrifying than anything he had ever seen. He couldn't even stutter a response but he managed, by closing his eyes, to shake his head.

'Do as you're told, moron. Get in the Van – now,' snarled the Dream Dealer, white froth beginning to form at the side of his mouth.

Flake, with his eyes still closed, folded his arms and refused to move.

'All right. I'll leave you here to explain to the Police who made the Ice-Dreams, who sold the Ice-Dreams and why two children are lying lifeless on the ground. Then who do you think is going to find themselves behind bars this very evening? Mmm, Flake? Answer me that.'

Flake opened his eyes and was immediately sucked into the slip-stream of the Dream Dealer's force.

'We're leaving now. Follow me.'

Like a sleepwalker, Flake walked to the Van and obediently climbed in. The Dream Dealer was concentrating so hard on keeping Flake within his control that he never noticed the determined little Earth-imp running from the Van towards Finn. She was dragging a plastic spoon.

Flake switched on the engine. The Dream Dealer glanced around the inside of the Van for his Earth-imp. She was nowhere. He looked through the window and saw her scooping some of the melting Mother-Dream Ice into the spoon. He watched admiringly as she heaved it across to Finn.

'Genius,' he thought, as she struggled to push the spoon towards Finn's slightly open mouth.

The Dream Dealer felt a peculiar warm glow in his reptilian body. That strangest of human feelings had taken root inside him. He loved her. Despite the way his outer body was reverting to its original shape, some small seed of goodness had been planted in that organ in his chest which was pumping the blood round his body. He picked up the oxygen mask and climbed through into the front seat where his precious, pulsating Jar was waiting for him. The rainbow colours had fused into a single, incandescent white light, shimmering expectantly, waiting to bring eternal life to its diabolic owner.

'Off we go, Flake,' he ordered. 'I'll be back for you later,' he shouted out to the little Earth-imp.

'I'm wwwaiting for you to p-put on your safety bbbelt, Bbbboss,' stammered Flake, playing for time.

'We don't need to worry about that. Immortal means you can't die, right, Flake?'

'There's D-Delphi,' cried Flake. 'Do you need her?'

'Drive on, idiot,' screamed the Dream Dealer, as he began attaching the tube to the Jar.

The Earth-imp had managed to balance the side of the plastic spoon against Finn's chin. She now jumped onto his face and started cupping the mixture into her hands, ready to shovel it into his mouth. Finn felt an odd tickling on his face and then the sound of the Van's engine start up. Though his head was spinning, he forced himself to his feet sending the Earth-imp, cursing, to the ground.

The Dream Dealer was going to escape and there was only one thought in Finn's head. He must stop him. As the Van began accelerating towards him, he jumped fearlessly onto the road in front of it.

Flake saw him and swerved away, losing control of the steering. There was a sound of screaming tyres, scrunching metal, smashing glass, as the Van crashed through the wall and into the Playground. The Jar flew out of the Dream Dealer's claws, through the windscreen and shattered into a thousand pieces. Lids exploded off the rows of stored bottles and waves of stolen souls escaped into the air.

Lights danced in Flake's head and everything went blank. He didn't see the Dream Dealer leap through the shards of glass and run towards the Earth-imp. Nobody saw two small, strangely shaped figures, with yellow eyes, running hand in hand into the distance.

The Broken Jar

Forks of coloured lightning streaked through the air. Children and grown-ups were thrown to the ground by the force of their souls re-entering their bodies.

Finn stood dazed, wondering whether this shower of fireworks was the after-effects of being knocked out. His head ached. There was a hole in the school wall. Kids were lying all over the street. Nothing made sense.

Delphi was the first to stir. For a moment she looked confused. Then she stood up and gazed in disbelief at the Ice-cream Van. The front was twisted, bricks from the wall lay all around it and its tinselly, tinkling tune was playing eerily over and over again. A small bottle, with Delphi's name engraved on it, lay shattered among the cigars and computer games. She had seen Finn jump bravely in front of the Van in an attempt to stop the Dream Dealer escaping.

But then she couldn't remember what had happened. She began to search around, trying to find Finn.

* * *

In the Art Room, Mr Turpentine sat up, presuming that he must have been knocked out by something falling from the ceiling. As he rubbed his head his wig slipped down over one of his eyes. He pulled it off and looked at it. Why was he wearing a wig? Who was he pretending to be?

He flung it into a nearby waste bin and strode out into the Playground. The first thing he saw was the crashed Van and he immediately hurried to see if there was anyone in it. Flake was slumped in the driving seat in a state of shock.

'Fred. Are you hurt?' Mr Turpentine said, looking with wonder at his old friend, Fred Lake.

Despite Flake's throbbing head everything was beginning to come into focus.

'Ben?' said Flake without any sign of a stutter. 'It's you, isn't it?'

Mr Turpentine nodded.

'How long is it? How long since …?'

'…since the day we met the Magician? Must be twenty years.'

'I remember watching you go,' said Flake. 'I felt so alone. You forgot all about me. Where did you go? What happened to you?'

'Indeed what did happen?' said Mr Turpentine miserably. 'All I know is I never painted another picture and I felt … I felt…I don't know how to describe it.'

'Try,' said Flake.

'I felt like…like I'd lost a bit of myself.'

Flake nodded.

'And you, Fred. What ever happened to you?' asked Mr Turpentine.

'It's all such a blur I can only guess at what happened. I fell completely under the Boss's spell. I lived on those hateful sweets and then those toxic Ice-Dreams. I lost more than a bit of myself. I'm not a person at all. I'm…'

Flake buried his head in his hands. The pain of remembering was too great. They sat in silence except for the insistent tinkle of the Ice-cream tune. Mr Turpentine finally switched it off and patting Flake on the back, said,

'That's the past now. Come on. Let's see to the kids. They may need our help.'

* * *

The children were beginning to sit up and look around. They were dazed but their eyes were alive again. Delphi was standing quietly beside Finn. He was lost in his own thoughts.

'Where am I?' said Scorcher. 'Where have I been?

It's dark. So dark down there. And spiders, spiders everywhere …' He began looking around agitatedly.

'You're okay, Scorcher,' said Delphi, going over to him. 'You've had a bad dream.'

Finn looked up at the sound of their voices and watched Delphi put her arm, comfortingly, round Scorcher.

'What's going on? Who brought me back?' continued Scorcher.

'Finn did,' said Delphi.

Scorcher stood up and walked across to Finn.

'Thanks, mate. What can I say? What…?'

'Sorry perhaps,' interrupted Delphi. 'You took all his money, spent it on a dream and nearly killed yourself.'

Scorcher looked incredulous.

'Finn's money? I couldn't have…his money for the dog?'

'Forget it,' said Finn quietly. 'It's not important now.'

'Course it is,' exclaimed Scorcher. 'Just wait till Mum and Dad hear you saved my life. They'll give you any amount of puppies…'

'No they won't,' cut in Mr Turpentine sharply, as he crossed the road with Flake. 'You will earn every penny of that money back yourself. Your first job will be helping mend this wall. Understand?'

Scorcher nodded his head. Then he noticed Flake and again remembered the nightmare.

'Where's the…? Where's the…?'

'Dream Dealer?' questioned Flake. 'He seems to have gone.'

'You did it, Fred!' exclaimed Mr Turpentine. 'You smashed the Van, smashed the Jar, smashed the…'

'You did it,' said Delphi quietly to Finn. 'I watched you jump in front of the Van. It was you who destroyed him.'

'He destroyed me. He destroyed my mother,' cried Finn, in despair. 'Tore her to shreds.'

'It was only a photograph,' said Delphi.

'IT'S ALL I HAD!'

Finn's voice cracked as he gave way to tears.

'Delphi!' shouted a woman's voice. 'Delphi, come here at once.'

The sight of the broken wall, the crashed Ice-cream Van, the group of children all standing around in shock, confirmed everything that enraged Delphi's mother about this school. Her whole face had turned pink, even her forehead. She was cursing the day she had ever discovered Yewton High School.

Delphi looked up and saw her mother striding towards her. Delphi's mother didn't often get angry but when she did, she was scary.

'We're getting out of here, now. Right now.'

'But Mum …' started Delphi.

'Do what you're told. I don't want to hear another word from you.'

Delphi's mum took her firmly by the hand and

started to drag her away. Delphi reached back towards Finn. Tears flooded her face.

'Delphi,' howled Finn, as he watched her being ripped away.

He curled up on the ground, wracked by silent sobs.

Delphi's mother stopped. Desperate as she was to leave this hateful scene, she could not walk away from a child in such distress.

'Wait here,' she ordered Delphi, as she headed towards Finn. She knelt down beside him and put her hand on his shoulder.

'Are you hurt?'

Finn shook his head. She rubbed his back, waiting until his sobs gradually slowed down and he finally inhaled a deep breath and was quiet.

'What's your name?' she whispered.

'Finn.'

'What?'

Her arm tensed, jolting him sideways.

'Finn,' he repeated.

'So what's happened…Finn?'

'Nothing…everything. I've lost…everything.'

He buried his head in his arm as waves of loss overwhelmed him again.

'Shall I ring your parents?'

He shook his head.

'Dad hasn't a phone.'

Delphi's mother stared into the distance. Wild

thoughts swept through her. She took Finn's head firmly in her two hands and looked hard into his crumpled face.

'Finn,' she asked. 'What is your surname?'

Finn dragged the back of his arm across his face and sniffed hard.

'Your surname. What is it?'

'Stevens,' he mumbled, his eyes and hands tight closed.

'Stevens?' she questioned. 'Are you sure? Are you sure it's not Finn ... Greenstock?'

'Greenstock?' thought Finn. 'Why did she care what he was called?'

He looked up. His eyes fastened on hers.

'We get letters saying Greenstock.'

She held his questioning gaze with a look of utter certainty.

'Dad says they lived there before us.'

'Finn Greenstock. It's you, isn't it? I know it's you.'

'Me?'

Finn stared and stared at her. The woman in the photograph?

'Who are you?'

She grasped him with both arms and held him so tight it almost knocked the breath out of him. Everything went dark. He was aware only of the sound of her heart beating in his head.

'Finn,' she said, her voice trembling. 'I am your ... your mother.'

He begged this moment to be true.

'Your birthday is May 30th.'

Yes, his birthday was May 30th. She knew. This was mum. This really was his mother. But how could this have happened? Only minutes ago he had lost, not just his precious photo of her, but every scrap of hope that he would ever find her.

He thought of how he had searched and searched and tried and tried and now – when he had failed completely, given up totally – she had appeared. Who was it once said that…someone once said, that, when you reach the point when you stop trying and give up – that's when it all happens. Who was it? Suddenly Finn remembered – the dreaded Dream Dealer. A shiver went through him. Instantly, he felt the enveloping warmth and safety of his mother's arms holding him. How many times had he imagined such a moment?

His tears fell and fell. Would they ever stop? The dam inside him, so carefully built over the years, had finally burst. Nothing mattered now. He had mum.

Delphi had come over and was watching them, silently. Her mother turned, her eyes too were filled with tears. But these weren't the tears that had made Delphi angry so many times before. Happiness was radiating from her mother, shining through her tears, like sun through rain. Delphi put her arm round her.

'You and Finn are twins,' whispered her mother. 'My twins.'

Delphi's arm tightened. She, who always had so many questions, stood speechless, gazing at Finn, her brother.

'Twins,' sniffed Finn, hoping that by repeating what she said, he could somehow make sense of her words. His mother nodded.

'Does that mean your Dad's my Dad?' said Delphi in a small voice.

Their mum nodded again.

'Twins! Finn, can you believe this?'

Finn shook his head.

'Me neither,' said their mum, one arm round each child.

Finn could never find the words to describe that moment. The sense of belonging and completeness. It was not just that he had found his mother, found his twin, but that the whole world felt like his mother – and every human in it felt like his brother and sister.

'So am I the gold you were looking for?'

'You,' she whispered, 'are my lost treasure.'

Meeting Up

Finn had long-since discovered that nothing ever happens as expected.

Yet another surprise was his father's reaction to the news. If Dad had lost it when Finn unearthed a photograph of Mum, what was he going to do when he discovered Finn had actually found the real live Mum and Delphi?

Dad listened quietly while Finn told him the story. His face expressed no more interest than if he were hearing about Finn's geography homework. He didn't ask a single question. He didn't even blink when Finn said Mum and Delphi were coming to tea tomorrow.

The next afternoon Dad suddenly announced that they'd better have a bit of a clear up. He set to work with the pile of dishes in the sink while Finn found a brush with half its bristles missing and had a go at sweeping the floor. Finn hated cleaning but this was fun. Dad started singing, 'Oom pah pah', to the clatter of plates.

'Maybe I'll be a cleaner when I grow up,' laughed Finn, leaning on his brush with a dishcloth over his head. He had managed to fill three black bin bags with rubbish and would have filled a few more if he could have found them.

When the kitchen was looking almost respectable Finn decided to have a shower. As the lukewarm water trickled through his hair and down his face, he wondered what Delphi would think of Dad. He so wanted her to like him.

'I've finished in the shower,' he shouted, as he rummaged through the clothes on the floor in his room, searching for a clean T-shirt. There was no answer from Dad.

'D'you get some milk, Dad? Or any biscuits?'

Still no answer. Had Dad gone out to buy some? Finn hurried into the kitchen, zipping up his trousers. He stopped, dread flooding through him. There was his father struggling to put a nearly empty whisky bottle back in the cupboard. He turned to Finn, his eyes dull and sorry.

'NO!' wailed Finn. 'Why didn't you say? Why can't you talk? I thought you were okay about it. You were singing just now. You're going to see your daughter, Dad. Doesn't that make you happy?'

There was a firm knock on the door. Finn

hesitated. Perhaps he should ignore it. Pretend they had forgotten.

'Pleeeeeease, Dad, act as if you're normal,' begged Finn, as he went to answer the door.

Mum was holding a big bunch of yellow flowers and Delphi was carrying a box that smelled like warm scones. Mum gave Finn a hug but he stood stiffly not sure what to do.

'We're all nervous,' whispered Mum.

'I was nearly sick this morning. I am so excited,' grinned Delphi. 'Show me where you found the photograph. I've been trying to imagine everything.'

Finn led them past the desk, pointing at it without looking. The smile went out of Mum's eyes as she glanced over the stained carpet and curtainless windows. Was this her son's home? She caught sight of Dad in the kitchen.

'John!'

Silence.

Mum looked at Dad, comparing him to the young man she had left. Dad kept his eyes on the table. She hesitated, unsure what to do next.

'Got a vase for the flowers?'

Still silence. She walked across the kitchen and opened a cupboard.

Dad stood up abruptly, his chair rocked but didn't quite fall.

'There's nothing in that cupboard,' he said sharply.

'No worries. It's all a bit of a shock, isn't it? Shall

I put the kettle on?'

The cupboard door stood open. The bottle of whiskey staring out of it. Dad grabbed it and held it against his chest as if willing it to protect him.

'No. Leave us alone. We don't need you. We don't need you to come along, smiling, as if nothing ever happened…we don't need you, do we, Finn? We're fine. We've managed fine without you, haven't we?'

Dad looked desperately across to Finn, hoping for support. But Finn stood frozen, immobilised by what was unfolding.

'John. It's all right, I …'

'You ran away. You left us. Now you think you can float back into our lives with a bunch of flowers and everything will be all right. Well, it isn't all right. Nothing's all right.'

He took the lid off the bottle and drank a big slug of whiskey.

'I know what you've come for. You're going to take Finn away. That's why you're here, isn't it?'

Mum's face had flushed red and her eyes glistened angrily.

'I hadn't planned to. But seeing you like this – drunk – a drunkard – living in this squalor makes me think maybe I should.'

This was worse than any nightmare Finn had ever experienced. It was like being in a torture chamber, pulled apart on a rack. He felt ashamed of his Dad and yet he hated seeing him attacked. He had never imagined his mother as anything but warm and loving and here she was breathing fire. He wanted to yell 'SHUT UP' to both of them but nothing came out of his mouth. His body was standing there in the kitchen and his mind was screaming in some other place where no one could hear it.

He felt a soft hand wrap round his scrunched fist. He looked at it. It was Delphi's. He had forgotten all about her. She pulled him into the other room. They sat down together on the green sofa. Furious words continued to fly like sparks from the kitchen.

'What was changing your name meant to achieve? Made you feel better, did it? Coward! Didn't you want to hear how Delphi was doing? Didn't you want …?'

'I wish she'd shut up,' said Delphi. 'Can't she see our Dad needs help?'

'Our Dad,' thought Finn.

'I can't believe what she's saying. It's nothing like what she told me last night.'

'What did she tell you?' said Finn, his body at last connecting to his voice.

'She was really nice about Dad. She said they'd met just after they left school.

She'd got pregnant and they'd moved into a flat together. Dad was studying at college and she stayed at home and looked after us. It must have been really difficult. They didn't have money and her friends didn't want to sit around changing nappies. Then she met Mike. He was working at the local hospital. He's a doctor. They fell in love and moved to Australia.'

'How old were we?'

'About a year, I think. She said she desperately wanted to take us both but it wasn't fair on Dad. Australia's so far away. He loved us both. He was a great dad, she said. So they kind of agreed that he'd keep you and Mum would take me.'

'Sounds fair,' said Finn unconvincingly.

He gently lifted Hercules out of his box and watched him run up his chest.

'Sure. If we'd been china ornaments. 'You have the swan, dear and I'll take the pig'.'

Finn chuckled.

'It might have helped if Mum had actually told me what happened,' said Delphi.

'All I ever wanted to know was whether I had a mum, whether she was alive or dead.'

Finn felt his throat tighten. He didn't want to cry. He stroked Hercules over and over with his thumb. Sometimes he imagined he was Hercules. Hearing everything, seeing everything, but nothing getting at him.

'Mum was always unhappy. But I keep thinking how hard it must have been for Dad. For both of you,' said Delphi.

'He should have married someone else like your – like Mum did.'

'Mum says he'd wanted to, but his girlfriend told

him that he had to choose between you and her.'

'Really!' exclaimed Finn, looking towards the kitchen.

He felt a surge of love for Dad, even if he was drunk.

'If only she'd told me the truth instead of going on about 'treasure' maybe we'd have found each other sooner.'

'One thing's certain,' said Finn. 'If I ever have kids, there are going to be no secrets.'

The shouting had stopped but Dad was crying. What's more Mum was crying too.

'So what happened to granpop,' Mum was saying between sniffs. 'I went straight to his place when we got here. They said he'd died.'

'Four years ago. Heart attack. He was the last of the family,' spluttered Dad.

Finn looked at Delphi. She rolled her eyes to the ceiling.

'Grown-ups!' she said. 'Let's go and sort them out.'

'I'm sorry, John. Neither of us did very brilliantly,' said Mum, as Finn and Delphi came into the kitchen. 'But we did manage to produce these two.'

Hercules's nose twitched in the air, then he licked his paws and began cleaning his face.

'I'm Delphi,' said Delphi.

Finn had never seen her look shy before.

'And I'm Dad.'

Delphi walked slowly across and put her arms round his chest. He kissed the top of her head and held her. The light had come back into his eyes.

Mum gave Finn a hug taking care not to squash Hercules.

'Let's make some tea. We've brought scones and cream and strawberry jam.'

May 30th

A year had gone by and Finn and Delphi were together on their birthday for the first time since they were one year olds. All their questions had been answered. There were no longer any secrets left festering in the dark.

'D'you remember this time last year, Mum?' laughed Delphi, as she put a plate of mini-pizzas into the oven. 'I stumped out of the house because you cried and embarrassed me in front of Scorcher.'

'I'll never forget. And what a miserable birthday Finn must have had. If only we'd known,' said Mum, placing a second cake, with 14 candles, on the table.

The doorbell rang and Delphi's stepfather went to answer it. It was Finn and Dad.

Following close behind them were the rest of the kids.

'Mum insisted I brought this,' said Scorcher, holding up a bottle of champagne. He rummaged in his knapsack and pulled out an unwrapped picture which he handed to Finn. It was an ink drawing of a spider. Finn studied it intently.

'It's really good…you've got every detail right…I can't believe you did this. Thanks so much.'

'It's beautifully drawn, Scorcher,' said Mr Turpentine, helping himself to a piece of cheese and pineapple. 'Though I'm a bit surprised at your choice of subject.'

Scorcher explained that, when he had been helping rebuild the Playground wall last summer, he had come across a spider's web with a huge spider hanging between the bricks.

'I was so terrified I couldn't go near the place. Then Finn told me everything about spiders and somehow they weren't so scary anymore,' explained Scorcher. 'Did you know they don't have ears? They hear with the teeny hairs on their legs.'

'You're joking!' exclaimed Meg.

'It's true, I swear,' said Scorcher.

'Certainly explains why I've got better hearing than Bela,' said Cal. 'My hairy legs!'

'Who's got hairy legs?' asked Mum, bringing in a large plate of sausages. 'Finn, can you pour Flake a glass of champagne - and one for me, while you're about it.'

Finn filled the glasses and then asked Dad what

he would like.

'I'll have one of those sausages, please, and a diet coke.'

'And I've got something for you, Dad,' said Delphi. 'It's the same as I gave Finn for his birthday. I thought you should have one too.'

She handed her father a smartly wrapped parcel. Dad opened it, taking care not to tear the paper. He took a deep breath when he saw what she had chosen to give him. It was a photograph of himself, Mum, and Finn and Delphi when they were babies. It was not the same as the one that Finn had found under the desk, but it had been taken on the same day.

It reminded him of all the darkness that had been in his life for so many years. He couldn't trust himself to speak but he gave Delphi a hug and concentrated on a shaft of sunlight that had fallen across the room.

'D'you like it, Dad?' asked Delphi.

Dad nodded, then said,

'I'm going to keep it on my desk at work.'

Bela and Trixie were teasing Turk about his orange T-shirt.

'It's so bright, I need dark glasses to look at you,' said Bela. 'But I suppose it's one better than Finn's freaky shorts.'

Finn chuckled.

'You call them old-fashioned, I call them retro! They've got great pockets.'

'D'you know I quite miss Hercules,' said Cal. 'You must really miss him, Finn.'

'I do. But he did well. Four years is a long mouse life.'

'At least there's not that awful piss-smell,' said Meg. 'But, I agree, I miss the mouse too.'

'Well, I don't,' said Mr Turpentine, scratching his bald head. 'I'll never forget the day he went up my trouser leg.'

'Have another sausage,' humoured Cal, looking over Mr Turpentine's shoulder at Turk who was standing, waiting.

He had a piece of paper on the end of his finger and as Mr Turpentine reached for a sausage, he swiftly stuck the paper on his head.

The children were struggling to keep straight faces. Mr Turpentine stood up and smiled at the kids. He took a swig of champagne and nonchalantly walked over to Dad.

'There seems to be a sticker on the back of my head, could you be very kind and read what it says.'

'*Endangered species*,' obliged Dad, in a deadpan voice.

'And indeed they are,' said Mr Turpentine. 'Only two hairs on a whole head is not many and I don't think they are going to breed – not even in captivity.'

Everyone laughed. At that moment the doorbell rang.

'I think it's our birthday present,' said Mum, as she and Dad went to answer the door.

Standing there was Alf carrying a puppy under each arm.

Finn and Delphi gasped as they saw first one puppy and then the other. Wide-eyed, they looked at each other across the room and grinned.

'Let me help you, Alf,' said Dad, taking one of the wriggling puppies and carrying it back into the room. 'It's one each, so you two will just have to sort it out between you.'

'Don't worry about it,' said Mum, 'the puppies will choose.'

Finn and Delphi were silent with excitement, their eyes transfixed by the loose-skinned little bundles of squirming fur. Alf and Dad put the two puppies on the floor and one of them immediately made its way to Finn. He knelt down on the floor and let it nestle under his neck. The other puppy clung round Alf's legs.

'It's shy, poor little thing,' said Delphi, as she picked it up.

'I can't believe this,' said Finn, looking up at his parents. 'Thanks so much Mum. Thanks Dad.'

'I guessed you might get Finn a puppy but in a million years I never thought you'd get me one as well,' said Delphi.

'It's too big to fit up your sleeve, Finn,' said Mr Turpentine.

'Or up your trouser leg,' added Meg.

'I'll need to get them back to their mother now,' said Alf. 'Give them another week and you can take them home.'

'I can give you a lift in my taxi,' said Flake to Alf. 'I've got to be going now.'

'Thanks, me duk, that would be a great help,' said Alf, gathering the two puppies into his arms.

'Why have you got to go, Flake?' said Delphi. 'You'll miss the cake.'

'I am being interviewed by Miss Pelly,' said Flake proudly. 'She wants to know about the scales and the bottles and the Jar.'

'The Yewton Myth,' said Finn. 'It's going to be a great story.'

'I like the bit about you,' said Delphi. 'The bit that says when the earth-imp chose to disobey Mother Nature and do something totally selfish, there was only one thing that could ever stop him. A child who would choose to do something totally unselfish. That was you, Finn. You did it!'

'I do wonder,' said Finn, 'whether I would ever have found Mum or discovered we were twins if it hadn't been for the Dream Dealer?'

Epilogue to the Yewton Myth

By Year 9 and Miss Pelly

'The question is what happened to the Dream Dealer and his little Earth-imp? His great scheme was temporarily in ruins but it seems unlikely that he returned to the centre of the earth. He was too enchanted by the life of humans and above all by their total disrespect for Nature and her laws. No doubt, he will find a way back and continue to wreak havoc and unhappiness. But there is also the possibility that he may grow to understand, as might the humans whose freedom he envies, that fighting Nature ultimately leads to self-destruction.

'Mother Nature knows that only by living in harmony with Her can there be eternal life.'

THE END

ABOUT THE AUTHOR

Marita Phillips is a lyric writer. She has written
the book and lyrics for the children's musicals:
'The Dream Dealer' and 'BUZZ – the story of
Glory Bee' (music by Harriet Petherick Bushman)
This is her first novel.

The Dream Dealer

a musical for schools and youth theatres
www.thedreamdealer.com

First performed in 2003, The Dream Dealer musical was awarded a Fringe sell-out show logo at the 2006 Edinburgh Fringe Festival and is currently performed worldwide.

Published by Next Gen Publications.
www.nextgenpublications.com/musicals-dream-dealer.htm

Stagecalls Theatre School, Exmouth 2010

"I produce about 15 shows each year, but I have to say working with 'The Dream Dealer' has been one of the most enjoyable projects ever. Everyone seemed to love working on it - and there were, more or less, 85 children involved - with a staggering age range of 4-16 years. The story-line/characters and music just seemed to appeal to everyone - which is quite unusual."

SAMANTHA OLIVER

Nagoya International School, Japan 2009

"Our school performed the Dream Dealer to rave reviews from parents, teachers and students. It was the best musical our school had ever put on. For me, it's so good to have material that has a relevant message to young people."

MATT HUGHES

You can order further copies of this book
direct from Neve Press.

To order further copies of **The Dream Dealer**
please send a copy of the coupon below to:

Neve Press,
53F Lancaster Gate,
London W2 3NA.

Alternatively, you can order online:
www.thedreamdealer.co.uk

- ✂

Please send me_____copies of The Dream Dealer.

I enclose a UK bank cheque or postal order, payable to
Neve Press for £ _____ @ £4.99 per copy.
(Plus £2 postage and packing)

NAME:
_____

ADDRESS:
_____

_____

_____
                                                 POSTCODE:

Please allow 28 days for delivery. Do not send cash. We do not
share or sell our customer's details.